HOMELAND

HOMELAND

edited by
Jon Gower

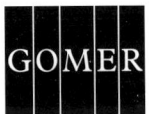

First Edition—November 1996

ISBN 1 85902 471 8

All rights reserved. No part of this book may be reproduced, stored in a retrieval system, or transmitted in any form or by any means, electronic, electrostatic, magnetic tape, mechanical, photocopying, recording or otherwise, without permission in writing from the Publishers, Gomer Press, Llandysul, Ceredigion.

Printed in Wales at
Gomer Press, Llandysul, Ceredigion

Contents

	page
Foreword: Dai Smith	6
Farming through the Decades: Patrick Dobbs	9
Taffy's Still a Welshman: Dylan Iorwerth	23
Living in a Language: Elin Rhys	36
Going Wild for Woodland: Malcolm Smith	52
Acid Drops of Rain: Simon Bareham	60
Life Down Under—Protecting the Marine Environment: Mike Gash	67
Ants in your Pants and Other Natural Phenomena: Jack Donovan	73
Village Voices: Noragh Jones	85
Wales: the People's Landscape: Madeleine Gray	102
Incomers: Mario Basini	118
Wales on the Map: Jon Gower	136

Sounding Off: Ian Skidmore

The Live People Export Trade	Hell on Wheels	20
An Eisteddfodic Tipple	Cats on Sugar Bags	34
'Phone Nuisances		51
Park Problems	Gun Laws	58
Farming the Wind	Well Meant Bad Advice	65
Canine Matters		72
Village Life, Village Death	Tele-Village Life	83
City Folk, Country Ways	Local Government	101
Museum Wales	New Authorities	116
The Poor Tax		133

Notes on Contributors	149
Acknowledgements	151

FOREWORD

The first time I left Wales I went through a tunnel. It was 1951. There was a Festival of Britain and the second Elizabethan Age was about to begin but it was a very nineteenth-century Wales I left, one aptly symbolised at the Festival by Paul Dickson's film *David*, in which the fomer miner and eisteddfodic bard, D. R. Griffiths, played the wise and sensitive school caretaker. D. R. Griffiths, of course, was the brother of Jim Griffiths, leading light of the about-to-fall Labour Government, which itself reeked of the dreams and achievements of my Homeland. And when, after a brief holiday with my own ex-miner grandfather, on the Kentish coast—where, for a Rhondda boy in 1951, the most wondrous thing was that a white shirt collar did not go black after a day's wear—we went home through that late Victorian tunnel, it really did feel like re-entering a more familiar world with its own distinctive landscape. Much of what I felt as different was a compound mixture of industrialised life and a culture, the experience of that historical process, which had made modern Wales such a pluralistic society—at once intensely local and rooted and cosmopolitan and diverse. In the years that then followed, and despite a passionate adherence to a still-thriving Welsh-language culture, much of that experience, and its attendant landscape, has been homogenised. If you leave Wales today by that tunnel or those bridges, if you cross our border with England at any point, or sail to Ireland or fly to Europe, the taste of difference is less and the shock of re-entry not so palpable. So much cannot be sensibly gainsaid.

Even so, the last decade and a half have also seen the Welsh emerge as one of the most self-conscious people within these island shores, and maybe beyond. We have quizzed ourselves, too much so some would say, about our shared and divergent history; we have argued a case for the articulation of our past and future destinies in both our tongues; and arguments for new political and social structures revolve like satellites in search of receiver dishes. Only the landscape, even if changed, remains. Or does it? Or rather, if it does, how do our human needs now relate us to that dramatically altered physical world which still holds us? Why are we driven to devastate what we must conserve if we are to leave room for life?

Some of the answers and most of the questions are to be found in the *Homeland* series which BBC Wales has broadcast weekly over the last three years. It has been a lively and challenging series which, at ease with itself and its audience, has focused on our common environment and our connected, urban and rural, Welsh lives. The proof of *Homeland*'s good sense, lack of pomposity and engagement with its one great subject, Wales, is now further established by the delight and the provocation of the essays in this book.

First, the country, then the films about the country, and now the book. But always, abidingly, the country, our Homeland—Wales.

Dai Smith
Head of Broadcast
BBC Wales

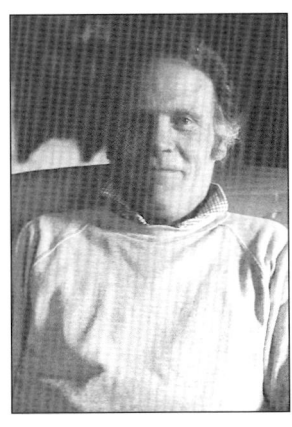

Farming through the Decades

A personal view

PATRICK DOBBS

It is afternoon in winter and I am driving along a narrow country lane in north Carmarthenshire. On my left is a small farm holding. Rusty corrugated iron sheeting flaps from the roof of the silo-barn, built in the 1950s with concrete breeze blocks and a £400 grant from the Min of Ag. The dwelling, smeared with the cement render obligatory for anyone after a council renovation grant in the 1960's, overlooks a yard littered with the detritus of abandoned hope—a seized-up tractor, a baling machine that has baled its' last bale and a retired wheebarrow in need of recuperative care. A couple of Holstein Friesian heifers, worth rather less in the market than the two sheepdogs riding in the back of my motor, gaze from the kitchen window in more hope than expectation at their untidy stack of damp hay. Three hens pick their way past paint tins and jam jars from the back doorway of the house to the cowshed entrance. The doors, both agricultural and domestic, never survived the winter before last. It is not a pretty sight—post milk quota, too small to compete, family fed up and gone away, marginal land farming where the drainage is bad, the fences and fixed equipment in disrepair and the holiday home potential poor.

Land hereabouts is cheap—well, relatively cheap—and property is always available. For half a century this has proved an irresistible combination to the idealistic and impecunious. 1950, and practical farmers were moving from rural England to little England beyond Wales in Pembrokeshire, in one of the great twentieth century farming migrations in the tradition of the moves from Ayrshire to Essex, from Devon to Kent, from Wales to Warwickshire and from East Anglia to Romney Marsh. At about the same time their less experienced urban cousins began a slow infiltration into the wetter parts of Wales, the land of the *wauns* and the *werns*, the cobs and the corgis, looking not for a farming life but an alternative lifestyle. They found it, and it was unsatisfactory. They and their children either endured a life of chronic drudgery and acute lack of money or else they had another income from another source—pony trekking, broadcasting, antique dealing, quota broking, selling saddlery or advice on organic agriculture or simply from investments and remittances from wealthier relations. In any event, as they came they mostly went. But their smallholdings remain, unfarmed and uncared for.

And as I drive along I pass other enterprises that have squeezed farming out of these steep-sided Carmarthenshire hills. The boarding kennels. The pony farms. They announce themselves to the world on a notice board, So and So stud or This and That dogs' hotel. The backs of their motors declare their interest—'Show Dogs in Transit' or 'Caution—Horses'. Why their dogs deserve a special mention while mine don't I can't say, nor how we can be more circumspect while following a horse-box than a cattle waggon. But that is not what such notices are for. They advertise, as clearly as the badge on a soldier's beret, what sort of people they feel they are and the values to which they subscribe.

This is an untidy countryside, verging on the squalid. The land of small milk producers gone sour, the good-lifers who found the life not so good as they expected, and the horse holdings and dog farms resting between one tedious round of summer shows and the next. I pull into an empty yard beside an empty house. The man has gone to work in a garage, his wife to some class, aromatherapy or something, which she finds important. The children are in school. I put my dogs round the sheep. My sheep. For I am one of the new aristocrats, a mountain sheep farmer.

We may as well admit it. Things, just now, are going our way. I'm driving round my winter grazings, in the only new vehicle I've ever had, and proving it. The sheep are everywhere, mine from Cardigan Bay to Salisbury Plain. Come summer they will crop the short grass below Llyn y Fan, known to authority as CL18, shorter still. And for every one of them, up to my quota and provided I fill in my IACS, my SAPS, my HLCA, my Continuous Flock Record, my Medicine book and my Animal Movement book and bury those that die and look after those that live and always gather them together to be counted at any time without notice, I will receive about thirty pounds in subsidy plus whatever I get from selling lambs and wool. No wonder I'm laughing. No wonder the suicide rate amongst farmers tops the table. Things are, quite definitely, not what they were.

Very curious. After seventeen years under a government committed to free enterprise and the free market our farming industry is more hemmed in with regulations and dependant on state intervention than ever before. But it is essentially financial control. Farmers are incensed that threats to human and animal health from sheep scab and BSE have been allowed to run riot through relaxing compulsory notification and treatment. Our incomes are now so linked to subventions that the principal relevance of product price is the effect it will have on CAP support in the following year. One of my earliest lessons in farm accountancy was that if the hen wasn't laying eggs there was nothing to put down and if she was there would be nothing to worry about. But the days of book-keeping on the back of an envelope have gone, and a quick appreciation of the possibilities of each new directive from Brussels is quite as important as knowing how to look after the hens—or even collecting the eggs.

But farmers are used to government policies which are out of tune with the political philosophy of the party in power. Who would have expected Labour ministers, committed one might have thought to the redistribution of wealth in favour of the less-well-off, to run the old Hill Farming and Farm and Horticultural Development Schemes? The benefits of both were specifically denied to those in a small way of business, as the opportunities for new entrants to the industry were reduced by their Farm Amalgamation Scheme. And gone too, thank goodness and the Tory government, have those ridiculous farm investment grants under which the rich were paid more than the poor for putting up new fences and sheds, drains and gates. Yes, a topsy-turvy world in which I have just been paid for planting broad-leaved trees on pasture that I reclaimed from deciduous woodland thirty years ago, helped of course by a whacking great subsidy!

In fact I'm into trees in quite a way of business. I have a hectare under the Woodland Premium Scheme, planted at the Forestry Commission's expense with oaks and ash, alder and rowan, beech, birch and cherry with a few larch-trees at the edge. Then there are a dozen or so clumps of trees, copses and extra-wide hedgerows ('wild-life corridors' in countrysidecouncil speak) which bring in a few pounds under the Tir Cymen scheme. And I musn't forget my nature reserve (Powys County Council pays for that one), my block of rough woodland fenced off for natural regeneration (Tir Cymen again) and my permissive path to the mountain (yes, good old Tir Cymen yet again).

I'm very environmental and all that, but what, that little bit of a farmer left in me might ask, has all this got to do with food production? If you send lambs to market you can count them, weigh them and grade them—but can you put a price on bird-songs and butterflies, or a valuation on a bank of blueberries? It has, of course, long been the case that if productive agriculture was closed down between the M4 and the Denbigh moors, and the investment diverted to better land in eastern England and northern France, the net effect would be to increase rather than diminish the total European food supply. It's just that farmers in Wales don't like to recognize it or be reminded of it. To those of us who've made a living in the market place through four decades it is very hard to adjust to an income from another source, however worthy. All those years ago we did, after all, choose a career in farming and not in the heritage industry.

Life is certainly easier nowadays, and not just because I've got a new landrover and central heating. The coming of the all terrain vehicle, which in any case I have not got, has given the farm bike only a short innings between the shepherding pony and the ATV. I'm a traditionalist, and still ride around on a horse. With only one of us left on the Black Mountain beside myself, and him even older than I am, if you see a man gathering his sheep on horseback take a good look, you may not see his like again. Llanybydder horse sale is not a place to meet so many farmers nowadays, nor do many of them still have a couple of cobs tucked away behind the house.

Machinery has become larger, more efficient, and very much more expensive. Most of my neighbours use contractors for the heavy work of silaging, now made in big bales with a plastic wrapper, and it is nothing to find forty thousand pounds worth of equipment trundling round the field. The hay harvest, which once lasted through June to the Royal Welsh Show day in the third week in July, is now literally wrapped up in a couple of days.

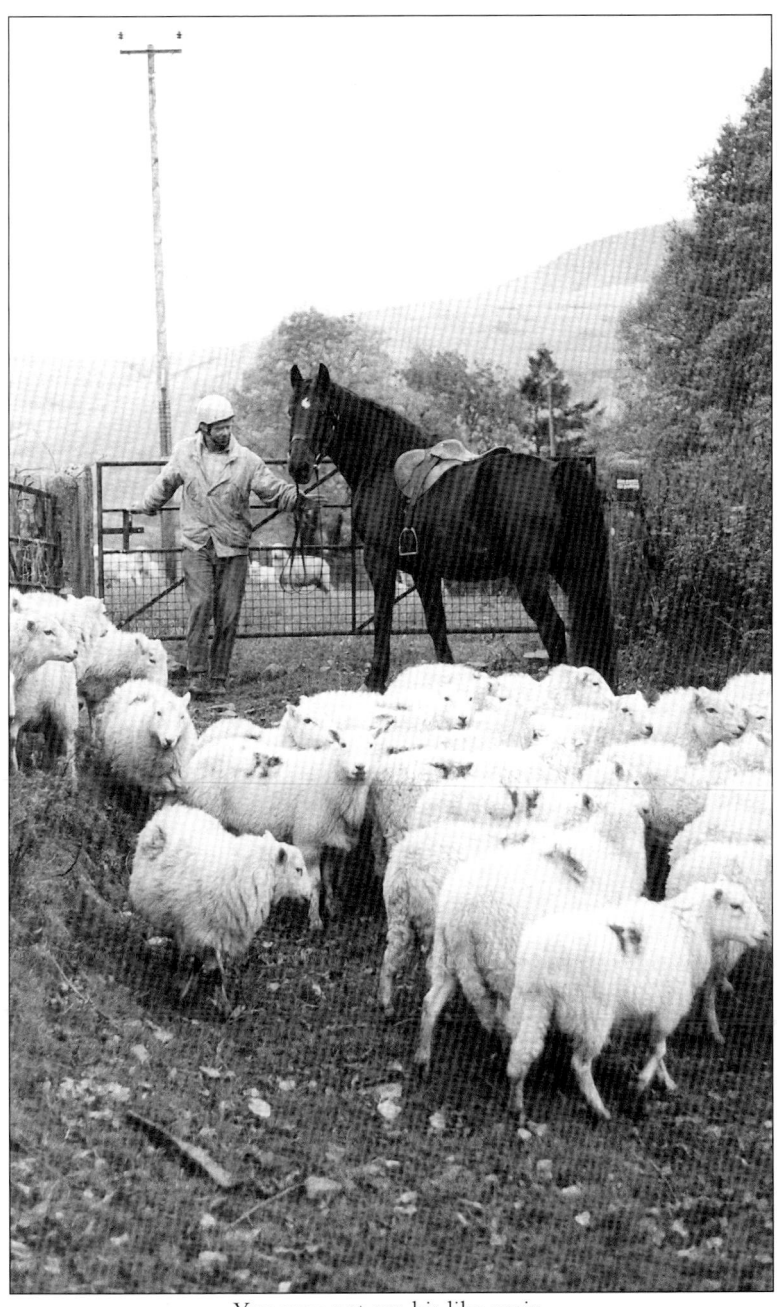

You may not see his like again.
(Photo: Erica Williams)

Because so much of their work was done under heavy subsidies in the 1970s and 1980s you don't see so many big diggers used for extensive land drainage schemes. Pastures are not limed so frequently and basic slag has to be brought all the way from Scotland following the cut-backs in steel production in Wales. Fields are no longer reseeded in regular rotation, so lambs are fattened off grass instead of rape. Docks, nettles and thistles, even ferns, are generally controlled by spraying, often behind the ubiquitous ATV.

Just as we no longer prepare for a long car journey by checking oil, water and tyres but just jump in and go so farmers expect their engines to work at the turn of a switch. We don't have the patience to tinker about with recalcitrant machinery any more. It's all too technical, and agents and agricultural engineers are fewer but far better equipped. An old cultivator you could take to the blacksmith to hammer together if it fell apart, but now a breakdown often means a journey of a hundred miles or more for service from a specialist. The yards filled with mowers and turners, ploughs and trailers which used to proliferate on the outskirts of every country town have mostly gone. Llandovery for instance, which once had three, now has no machinery agents at all. We put in a special order with a dealer perhaps as far away as Hereford or Haverfordwest.

Livestock farmers have an ever more effective armoury of drugs to control parasites and infectious diseases. When we relied on carbon tetrachloride to control liver fluke we dosed our ewes once a month from October until the hard spring frosts, but now we use something so powerful they only need a couple of shots. Antibiotics are targetted, and there are vaccines unheard of a decade ago. We can, at a price, keep more and more animals which in turn have to contend with ever more virulent strains of disease. But if you think livestock farming is high tech and highly subsidised travel to the arable areas of eastern England, where satellite monitoring to assess fertilizer, pesticide and herbicide needs of individual growing crops in individual fields, or even parts of fields, is becoming routine and EEC support payments are measured not in thousands but in tens and hundreds of thousands of pounds per farm.

And what of those whom the high-tech revolution has passed by, who have no quota for sheep or milk, who by living on the wrong side of an arbitrary line on a map are ineligible for 'conservation' grants and 'environmental' support? Scan through the classified advertisements of farming magazines and there are plenty of alternative enterprises—milk sheep and water buffalo if you dare to milk them, ostriches, emu, farmed venison and wild boar if you're into exotic meats, llamas, alpacas and angora goats (or is it rabbits?) if you're tired of shearing sheep. Unfortunately my memory goes back to rabbit pie meat, magic biscuits, dairy goats and the old liberal party—all perpetually on the brink of the breakthrough that never came.

Things, as I may have suggested already, have changed. We cannot as farmers, for instance, assume as we could a decade or so ago that the sheep farming interest was the only legitimate interest in Llanddeusant, on the principal that what's good for General Motors is good for America. When we selected a committee to purchase our local school for community use names were suggested on the basis of 'relevant skills' rather than ancestral identity with the parish and a social conformity that pre-dates political correctness. A revolution indeed. In the public arena farmers are weaker than they used to be, and they know it. Farmers' Union presidents have nothing like the influence of the late Jim Turner, Lord Netherthorpe, and in Wales we are still divided. The Farmers' Union of Wales and National Farmers' Union provide a duplicated network of branches and committees, so twice as many farmers can play some small role on the stage of public events, which presumably gives them some self-satisfaction and is unlikely to do the rest of us a great deal of harm. Competing too, to some extent, are a host of relative newcomers to agri-politics like the Highland Shepherds' Council and the Tenant Farmers' Association.

As political expression has become more pluralist the market has degenerated into an oligarchy of buyers. Small butchers purchase through wholesalers, as EEC regulations have closed the small abattoirs they owned or that supplied them. Supermarkets and multiples dominate the trade, so serious producers are as much concerned with uniformity as quality. A few enterprising souls have tried, sometimes successfully, to sell manufactured products such as 'farm-house' cheeses or 'home-cured' hams, but because their costs are high and their turnover low their food, which may be fit for the Gods, is eaten exclusively by the affluent middle class. The organic farmers, with their bogus science and misleading propaganda, still like to believe they occupy the moral high ground, and are still ignored by the overwhelming majority of farmers and consumers alike. Opportunities spring up from time to time such as the trade in very small lambs for Italy and Spain. These markets are seasonal and unreliable, so wholesale butchers hesitate to commit facilities to supply them and many of these lambs (but not my own!) are exported alive. Popular agitation against this practice is just one aspect of the increased interest by outsiders in what farmers get up to.

Ours is a very public occupation We don't work behind closed doors but out in the open-air. If we spread evil-smelling sewage-sludge on the land or work with noisy machinery at the weekend our neighbours may complain. If we leave a dead ewe lying around some passing hiker may have a word with the local Environmental Health officer. If a ram's horn curls round to press aganst his own head the RSPCA may be after us, and the regulations relating to the transport of animals are so complex that half the inspectors don't understand them. As food passes through more hands and undergoes more processes between the farmyard and the plate people become more aware of the hazards along the way, and more particular about how it is produced. As I write the BSE crisis is unresolved, but one thing certain to come out of it is that controls on food production will become tighter and tighter. More and more of the drugs we need can only be obtained from veterinary surgeons, and stringent and expensive product testing has excluded many well-established and inexpensive remedies because without a patent it isn't worth anyone's while to get them licensed.

The combination of labyrinthine regulation and high subsidies has soured relations between farmers and the field officers sent out to count sheep and cattle and check that farmers are keeping their multiplicity of records up to date. Years ago the National Agricultural Advisory Service, there to help you, worked closely with the administrative agencies, there to check up on you. But now the Agricultural Development and Advisory Service has been hived off. You pay for advice if you want it, and executive office staff have been instructed not to give it free, partly to avoid unfair competition with ADAS and partly because of the risk of perhaps huge liability if they get it wrong. So the field officer, once something of a father-figure, counsellor and friend, is now a policeman, even a spy. Individual members of staff, often born into the farming community themselves, are as helpful as they are allowed to be. They work very hard, but staff cuts have left fewer of them, with little time for the problems of individual farmers. Modern technology is all over us. Satellites in the sky monitor changes in our field boundaries and see we aren't growing potatoes when we've said we're growing grass, or cannabis anywhere at all. And we suffer along with everyone else from the curse of computers—marvellous when they work properly, but absolute swine when they wrong.

As the world moves on farming and country life moves with it, and we are as much victims of the social problems of the 1990s as our urban relations. They say the M4 provides a gateway and a getaway for thieves, and the drug culture makes theft a way of life from which some people apparently have to escape. Twenty years ago I never bothered to lock my house, ten years ago I would leave the keys in my motor at the mart in case anyone wanted to move it to get by. This year I have put locks on my tool shed and paid for a week's welding and woodwork to make secure barn doors. My horses are freeze branded and my machinery post coded.

Travellers and tourists have been moving amongst us for a long time. Hikers and Youth Hostellers, with whom may be bracketed for agricultural purposes the members of the Royal Society for the Protection of Birds and the Ramblers Association, are still regarded by many of my neighbours as dangerous subversives with their eyes on a mass take-over of the country. Many of them are genuinely puzzled to find that although they kept to the path and their dog on a chain they were still unwanted, while the followers of the hunt, haring around where they please as their hounds race loose over fields beyond the horizon, are generally tolerated and often made welcome. What these innocents do not understand, of course is that they are not and never will be *un o ni*—one of us—and the hassle is not at all about loss or damage but all about power—who has the right to control what goes on in the countryside. At a meeting of our Manorial Court E. J., one of the most respected flockmasters in Wales, when referring to a letter from the Brecon Beacons National Park Authority commented without risking any dissent, 'These people have too much power'. Those who were born, live and work in this place, whose dead lie generation on generation in the parish graveyard, cannot accept that others have a right to share in what they regard as their own. It is a fight which Welsh farmers wage as hard as Unionists fight for Ulster, but which they too know they will eventually lose.

Now that those great nomads the tinkers and Gypsies have for the most part been condemned to stay on permanent sites for itinerants (and there's a real cavortion of the language for you) grudgingly provided by a number of local authorities, the new bogeymen are the New Age travellers. I cannot recall anything that has ever united this community and all the villages and towns round about so nearly completely as the threatened arrival of these unwanted visitors in the early 1990s. Great boulders were left along roadside verges to prevent vehicles leaving the tarmac, gateways were obstructed with heavy implements and outsized tree-trunks, foul-smelling slurry was spread over small commons to deter anyone lingering there. Vigils were the order of the day and night. The police seemed more concerned with the safety of the travellers than the security of the residence, who were clearly more than capable of looking after themselves. Even the hippies in Tipi Valley were fearful of the New Age travellers. Nor would their fears seem to be unjustified, for they left behind them stolen property, burnt fence posts and a dead child.

However hard the farming community may rail against any perceived threat to their social and economic order we too are part of modern society. Our children are rebellious, our relationships stormy. Divorce, the ultimate disaster for farming businesses, strikes the most unexpected marriages. The greatest threat to traditional Welsh family farming comes not from political, economic or technical change but from the disintegration of traditional patterns of family life. Those who have been brought up to the drudgery, monotony and penury of small scale family livestock farming often want none of it.

Of my nearest neighbours three married late and have no children, another has a daughter married to a successful builder and my own children have professions of their own which take them flying round the word on stratospheric salaries. Farming in Welsh rural communities is burdened with a load of cultural claptrap and sociologial nonsense, sanctimonious, narrow, inward-looking and authoritarian and quite inconsistent with modern life which is urban, mobile, cosmopolitan and easy going. Because the demand for land prices is way above its value as a revenue earning asset it is often very difficult to pass a farm intact from one generation to the next if there is more than one child. Our government has refused to offer older farmers (and the average Welsh hill farmer has now passed his fifty fifth birthday) the pensions available to our contemporaries in Ireland and mainland Europe. The complications of transferring land, sheep and quota without losing ewe premia are so great that satisfactory partnership or share farming arrangements as are common in New Zealand seem to be impossible. It is therefore very difficult for a farmer to retire without giving up his home and all that he has worked for throughout his life.

The land remains. In ten, fifteen, or certainly twenty years time my neighbours and I won't be around and our children, those of us that have any, will have gone their separate ways. But these hills, these fields and woods will still be here, for all to see how we have cared for them in our generation. *Lector, si monumentum requiris, circumspice.*

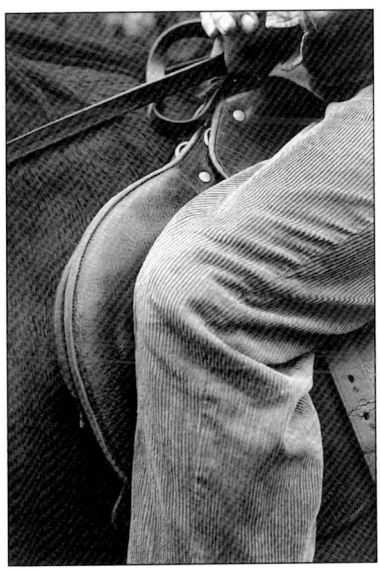

(Photo: Erica Williams)

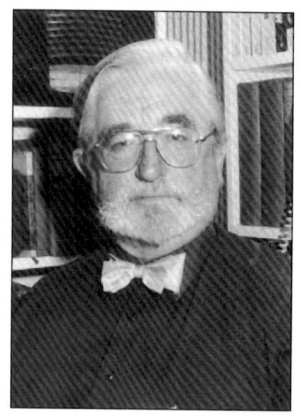

SKIDMORE SOUNDS OFF ABOUT . . . THE LIVE PEOPLE EXPORT TRADE.

I was talking to a farmer the other day on land his great-grandfather rented from the squire, just as he does. It is a fine farm. The keep for the cattle is grown on the place. He doesn't export live bull calves. He grows them on to fat and a few weeks ago he sold one for £700. Compassion in World Farming would love him. They might even massage HIM with a little compassion. He could use it.

His two sons were in the yard unloading the fertiliser which seems to be the only thing the farm buys in. They won't be there very long. He doesn't export calves. But he does a roaring export trade in children. Both are emigrating to Canada. They see no future in farming in Britain with its endless form filling and food wasting. We all know youngsters who graduate from agricultural college and a year later are still looking for a job. A farm of their own? Forget college. Buy a lottery ticket.

There was a time when a youngster could get his foot on the first rung of the farming ladder by renting a farm. Either from one of the estates or from the council. There are very few estates left and the number of councils with smallholdings to let are diminishing. Fortunately many of them are in Wales. But don't hold your breath. Local government is changing. The old paternalist non-political attitudes of the rural district councils—made up mostly of farmers —vanished with the councils themselves. English councils sell every scrap of land they can lay their hands on and it is too much to hope our Welsh councils won't follow that lead.

So what is left? Buying family farms. And you need very deep pockets to do that. The average farm of 130 acres is going to cost up to £3000 an acre. Every cow you put on it is going to cost you at least £400. The price of machinery? You plough the fields and scatter the pound notes round the banks. Little wonder my farmer friend's two sons are packing their bags and heading for the Canadian prairie.

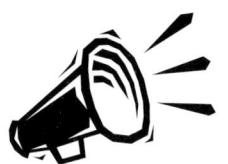

SKIDMORE SOUNDS OFF ABOUT... HELL ON WHEELS.

I do not encourage house guests. I believe in the Maori teaching in the matter—'Eat Up. Guests May Arrive.' If I did invite some one to stay with me, though, I would not be best pleased if they turned up with their bed and their three piece suite on a handcart. When you stay anywhere good manners dictate that you use what is on offer. You don't bring your home comforts with you. Yet people think nothing of coming here on holiday, dragging their homes behind them like badly designed snails.

Caravans. I would outlaw the caravan. Slums on wheels. Lovely inside, I grant you; if you like living hanging from each other's earlobes. Yet definitely not lovely to look at. And not a cheap holiday. Bed and breakfast at an admirable guest house which would really help the local economy is so cheap here it is practically free.

And I must say a man who buys a caravan cannot think much of his wife. What loving husband would insist his spouse includes in her holiday packing a sink and the kitchen stove? Look at it sensibly. He has a great holiday, the kids are free to frighten the farm animals. But the wife? Not only does she continue with the thankless tasks she performs every day, she leaves at home the labour saving devices which make her life bearable. Fridges so small you have to freeze ice cubes one at a time and no freezers. Everything prepared on the spot. No driers or washing machines. Lots of fresh air, though. Hanging out the laundry you have just hand-washed in a sink the size of an eye dropper. Caravan wives always have to go to the same place for their holidays . . . The 19th century.

You know what Hell is? Hell is waking up in the early morning on a bed that was designed for sideways sleeping; with the rain playing drum solos on the tin roof; with a full bladder and the terrible awareness there are two muddy fields between you and the bathroom. Hell is tramping across a Welsh tundra with your toothbrush at the high port. Looking forward to the sheer horror of sharing your bathroom with twenty strangers. Most of them breaking wind.

I wouldn't mind but they know they are not going to enjoy it. If you don't believe me, pay a visit to your local traffic view. Look at the expressions of the people in the front seats of the car. The stations of the cross framed in windscreens.

Taffy's Still a Welshman

DYLAN IORWERTH

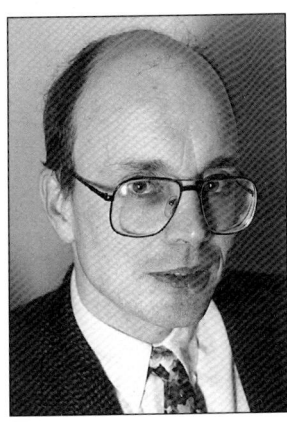

There I was, dreaming of far away sun-tans and of Mediterranean prawns the size of Dexter cattle. Holidays. Another chance to broaden my horizons and girth, an opportunity to see new cultures and to bring back another piece of fine art—a leprechaun with a shillelagh, perhaps, or a bull with a sombrero. And, of course, language.

Being the conscientious minority language speaker that I am, the multilingual phrasebook is as vital a part of the holiday kit as the immodium tablets. For a committed Welsh-speaker, travel is the opportunity to learn a smattering of someone else's language and to bore them with interminable monologues about his own. The first phrase to learn, obviously, is 'No, I am not English, I am Welsh'. You should not be deterred by the fact that the answer is usually, 'Bobby Charl-ton?'

An enterprising company from somewhere near Bala has been printing T-shirts in various languages for Welshmen and their progeny to wear on their summer holidays. 'I am not English, I am Welsh' they say bravely in a selection of European languages. A wonderful idea, especially for pickpockets and muggers who no longer have to work out whether you are a tourist or not. But enough of this lack of trust in fellow human beings . . . Hugo's 'Catalan in three months' is an admirable little book. In my case, the three months happen to be January, June and December but, apart from that, I had very few complaints, until I tried to work out that favourite phrase of mine. 'English' I found in the vocabulary at the back, opposite the page with 'Great Britain'. 'Ireland' and 'Irish' were a page further on and 'Scotland' towards the back. 'Wales' and the 'Welsh' weren't there.

For a man who prides himself on saying 'Catalunya' rather than 'that bit on the top right hand corner of Spain', this was extremely galling, on a level with that famous line in the Britannica Encyclopaedia, 'For Wales see England'. Despite having seen newspaper reporters, John Redwoods and football commentators all saying 'England' and 'Britain' as if they meant the same thing, it was still a shock to see that Wales did not exist in a book on one of our sister minority languages. Hadn't they heard of Bryn Terfel? Or even Max Boyce?

Most of the world hasn't. For most of the world, Wales isn't. I imagined flying off on my holiday, spending a wonderful fortnight toning up my skin cancer and then driving back from Heathrow along the M4, with a beautiful sulphur sunset gilding the smokestacks of Avonmouth. And then the Severn, the Sabrina of John Milton, and, beyond the gleaming, almost fluorescent river . . . bugger all. The phrasebooks had become reality, Wales had gone.

The most famous film about Wales is probably *How Green Was My Valley*, with its miners singing 362 part harmony on their way to work. John Ford's version was made more than 50 years ago and depicted events that took place another half century earlier. It was the coalface that launched a thousand sketches—comedians, who thrive on using shorthand stereotypes, love this image of Wales while Welsh actresses have built careers on method tea-pouring and bara brith slicing.

Even now, in the 1990s, when How Green Are My Wellies would be a better title, the BBC's Lottery programme chooses to show Wales as a land of coal mines and male voice choirs. If they find real coal mines, they should let the dole office know, but that should be easier than finding a male voice choir which is not off on a trip to Germany or the U.S. These days, of course, television producers have to set their programmes in museums to get the authentic image.

Poor Anthea, or whatever Lottery presenters are called, may not have known it but she was acting out a 1990s version of an event which has been happening for at least two hundred years. It used to be romantically minded travellers and poets braving a wild, mountainous country and writing diaries about it all; today we have blow-dried presenters bringing their advanced television technology and excitement to out-of-the-way locations. Just as those travellers' diaries were written for the amusement of friends and relatives back in civilisation, the viewer sees the strange and quaint natives through the eyes of familiar television personalities who are in their homes every week.

This is the television of the parachute news reporter who drops in on a story with a thousand anoraks and a hundred different hats. When he visits a coal mine, he has a helmet and lamp; aboard ship, he puts on a sou'wester; for a soccer story, he pulls on a fluorescent track-suit. We should be grateful that such reporters are not often sent on stories to transvestite bars and are only now and then despatched on a mission to remote and inaccessible parts of rural Wales. Parts that are so remote and inaccessible that only a few million tourists are able to find them each summer.

This is the television world that looks on everywhere outside south east England as the regions. There is evidence that it rankles with other parts of the smother country; for would-be nations like Wales, it is even more disturbing. But, like everything under the Sun, including that paper's informative article on Ten Things You Didn't Know About Welshmen and Sheep, it is not new.

The idea of outsiders coming in is central to Wales' image. Books, films, even postcards, tend to have been produced for a non-Welsh audience. Many of the television plays and films have been made by non-Welsh personnel—the BBC, S4C and HTV have all brought in big names from outside to try and make their products attractive to the network and US of A. In one memorable film based in the Teifi Valley, Edward Woodward was asked to play a part in Welsh without understanding a word of it. He gave us a glimpse of what would have happened if the Daleks had been on an Wlpan.

Karl Francis, the best known Welsh television and film director, who by 1996 had been appointed head of drama at BBC Wales, has called this 'blacking up'. The Red, Green and White Minstrels are alive and high-kicking throughout the television industry—one step forward from the numerous network decisions to replace Welsh characters with more sexy regional ones. We have had other major stars acting North Walians with a pseudo Rhondda accent, in a tradition that goes back to the early days of cinema in Wales. In his fine book on the subject, journalist Dave Berry points out that, up to the Second World War, all the major documentaries about Wales had been made by outsiders and most films had been manipulated to suit the needs of the box office and an outside audience.

As usual, the supreme example of the genre is *How Green Was My Valley*. Located in America and filmed with Irish actors, its director John Ford shrugged off concerns about accuracy with the memorable phrase, 'They're all Micks aren't they'. To Western eyes, orientals look the same; to major nations, minorities are monochrome.

Today's colonial traveller is A. A. Gill, aptly named after a motoring organisation. In the *Sunday Times*, he first chose the late 20th century's touchstone of good taste and manners, fancy food, to vent his bowels on Wales. Much of his gastronomic column was concerned with the strangeness of a country which has two languages but no cordon bleu tradition. Later, spurred on gleefully by the indignation of the fatwa-flinging Ayatollahs of Gwalia, he turned his elegant style onto Taffy's inability to recognise principles even if sheep wore them as underpants. For a metropolitan food writer, Wales is still uncivilised, although one suspects that he would not recognise laver bread even if it were smeared over his naked body and licked off by a Border Leicester.

In 1995, the art historian Peter Lord published a book about the way Wales was shown in cartoons and articles in the popular press between 1640 and 1860. It shows clearly how farming practices have changed—instead of today's jokes about sheep, there used to be jokes about goats. Otherwise, the stereotype of Welsh people is still recognisable—whining windbags, who like leeks and toasted cheese, a rowdy rabble who are almost always drunk and, of course, shifty. The English only waited less than a century after the invention of the printing press to publish the first accusations of this kind and have been at it for 450 years since then.

Peter Lord sums it up in his book, *Words With Pictures*: 'The conventional Welsh person first appeared in English literature, fully equipped with toasted cheese, leeks and a reputation for dirt and dishonesty, in the early sixteenth century' . . . he suggests that there must have been a long history to the stereotype for it to be so perfectly formed. Significantly, the title of this chapter in the book is 'A View from the Outside'.

In 1996, another academic, E. G. Millward, published a book of postcards about Wales from the early years of the 20th century. The images had changed slightly and the humour was less aggressive than in those days when bundles of rags used to be waved out of English windows on St. Taffy's Day, but most of the cards still showed primitive Wales through the eyes of a sophisticated traveller. The English visitor is invariably in plus fours and a motor car, the Welshman in mud and a cart.

One of the most interesting elements in these cards is the subdued use of sex, that major expression of the imperialist's power and fear. The nubile but coy Welsh girls are ripe for seduction; their innocence, naivety and strange language seems to make them a greater challenge and, behind the coded respectability of Edwardian Britain, there is a clear message about thrusting English men and yielding Welsh wenches. The Welshman's supposed bestiality is the obverse picture, like the white man's irrational fear of the black slave's sexual prowess or the protestant's persistent depiction of randy monks and nymphomaniac nuns.

As with the image of Wales, such images arise out of the power relationship between the two sets of people, the image-wielders and image-sufferers. This is the interface that could launch a thousand theses, but the strength and virulence of the image seems to reflect the varying levels of scorn and fear on one side, submissiveness and threat on the other. In the media exchange between Wales and England, an added complication is the insistence of the subjugated nation to retain its own language and culture which, by definition, shut out the conquerors. This is Groucho Marx inverted—everyone wants to be a member of a club which keeps them out.

For centuries, most English people would only have come across Welshmen when they ventured into England, as cattle rustlers, cattle drovers or possibly as rabble-rousing supporters of their own king, Henry VII. It was not until three centuries later that a tour of Wales started becoming a holiday possibility for the daughters of the idle rich and people of artistic temperament.

These were the days of the noble savage, when Thomas Gray could write of the Welsh Bard strumming his harp on the perilous heights of the mountain and lamenting a long-lost prince. Fittingly, the poem ends with the bard throwing himself off the edge and into the Celtic mist. While many of us wish that more Welsh poets might have followed his example, that image sets the scene for a century of image-making.

Later, and still sympathetically, the Welsh novelist Allen Raine—Anne Adeliza Evans—became the first pulp fiction bestseller and three of her novels were adapted for the screen between 1915 and

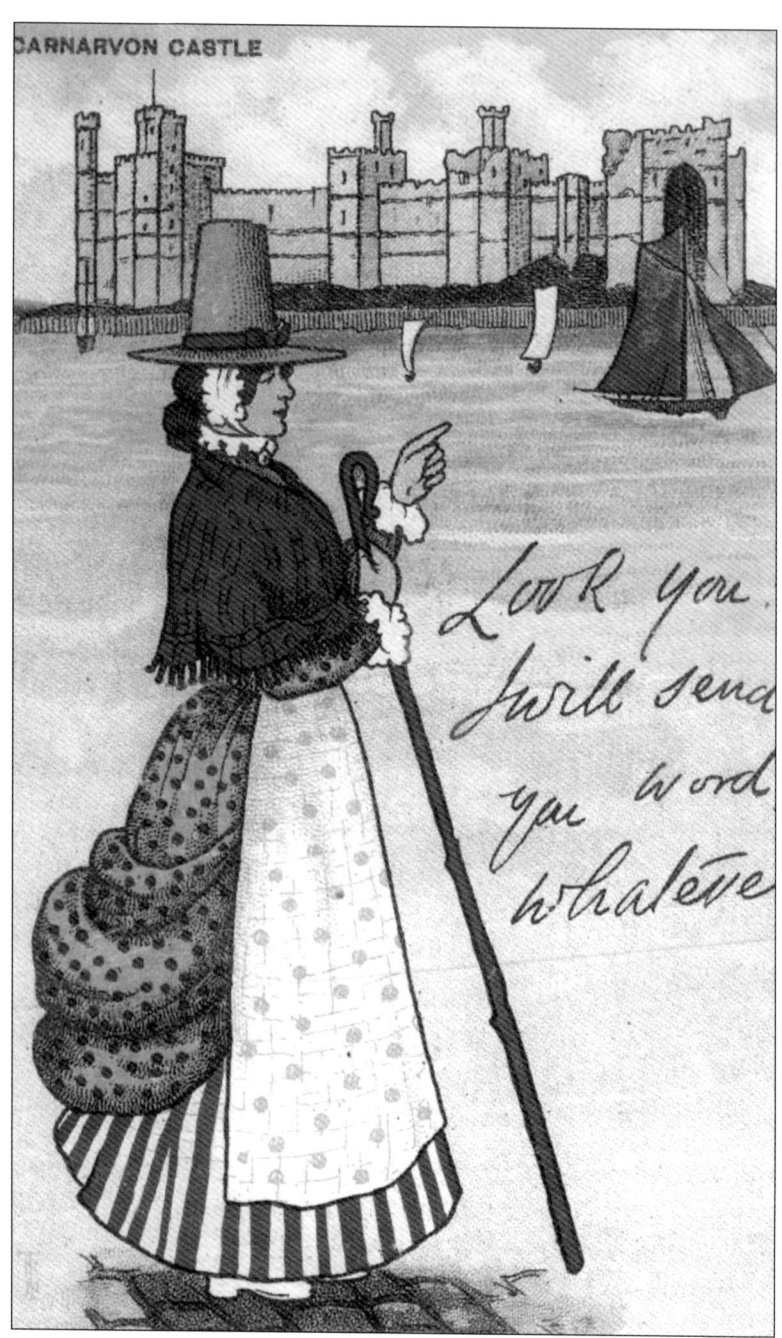

She's a card—'the subdued use of sex'.

1920. Dave Berry's book, as usual, draws out the salient points of one of the most famous of these, *The Welsh Singer*, where Myfanwy and Ieuan both escape out into the English world through their exceptional talents. The titles of films which followed suggest that Wales was treated in the cinema much as Enid Blyton did when her Famous Five visited Snowdonia: *Witch of the Welsh Mountains*, *Gwyneth of the Welsh Hills*, *Betta the Gypsy* and *Love in the Welsh Hills*. Later, the noble savage became the noble miner and Myfanwy became Mam. *How Green Was My Valley* was typical again in that it showed Wales as living in another age. Any conflict is distanced or smothered by male voice singing. Scottish commentators have noticed the same tendency in their industrial films—conflict either ends in peaceful accommodation between master and worker or is overtaken by a romantic story involving the main characters. Possible subversive characters are turned into jokes and, like black people or the American Indians, Welsh people are allowed to succeed and be heroes in bygone ages or in fields that aren't of vital importance, like singing, or very occasionally, rugby.

Another thesis could be written on the depiction of Wales in wartime. Shakespeare allowed Fluellen to be gallant and likeable while serving in the English army and there have been other Taffs holding their end up in war films, including *Zulu*. In 1943, the small village of Cwmgiedd was used as a propaganda substitute for a mining community in Czechoslovakia, where 173 men were shot by the Nazi occupiers. According to Peter Lord, the Welsh were heroes too when Jemima Niclas and her chimney-hatted, red-flanneled women from Fishguard frightened off Napoleon's army back in 1797. The past is the one place where Welshmen can really win. Owain Glyndŵr can still be a hero, much as Rob Roy or Bonnie Prince Charlie in Scotland. Period costume is a great help in relieving tension and it always helps if the Welsh are gallant losers.

In modern film and television, the main focus on Wales has been through the eyes of outsiders coming in, or long-lost Welshmen coming back. Even *How Green Was My Valley* has a distant perspective. It starts with the man looking back to the valley of his childhood, the valley which he has left. A typical scene—from an actual programme—would show an exiled middle-aged Welshman, who seems English in all but name and an ever-so-slight lilt, travelling by train back to his native Wales. His home village is in a timewarp, his relatives are as cheerful as happy hour at the local undertaker's and his father a bed-ridden rogue who hides his morals under his nightshirt, along with his whisky bottle.

This is the country of frightening village pubs where gap-toothed farm hands turn round to glare at visitors over their frothing pints. It is the country of former Welsh Secretary John Redwood's nightmares where natives in country shops turn from English to Welsh when a stranger walks in the door. It is the country of the half-man, half-goat kissing the fairy princess in the cartoon of 1796.

There have been other travellers; hundreds of thousands of them. Welsh people who left Wales to make their fortune in England. When Henry Tudor became King of England, they were there in droves, as triumphant as a rugby trip from Abercwmboi to Twickenham in the 1970s. Peter Lord's researches found Shon-ap-Morgan and Unnafred Morgan travelling up to London in 1747, each aboard a goat. Ealing producers after the war found actors Meredith Edwards and Hugh Griffiths stumbling off a train with red and white scarves, an uncontrollable harp and a druidic way with words and bushy eyebrows.

One of the classic Welsh films and plays is *The Corn is Green*, by the Welsh speaking Welshman, Emlyn Williams, whose life and fiction are uncannily similar. His main character is a young Welsh boy who is enlightened by an English woman and, through his talent and his acquisition of her language and manners, gets the chance to escape from his narrow background. This is Dr Look You Doolittle or even an early version of the Richard Burton story. Emlyn Williams once said, 'Rural Wales is where I belong, but I don't want to live in it. I want to have it to go back to.' Many of the issues in the debate over Taffydom reflect the broader tensions between rural and urban life, the region and the metropolis and class distinctions; it is the political context that makes them more acute. These days too, when image is all, trade bodies like the Welsh Development Agency and Wales Tourist Board believe the stereo-types damage Wales' chances. Some even suggest that the boyo image may have damaged Neil Kinnock and Labour's hopes in the 1992 election—an image which was typically painted by those non-Welsh Welshmen Michael Heseltine and Michael Howard.

For the rest of us, there are issues of power, democracy and fairness, particularly when faced with an ever-increasing and accelerating mass media. In 1995, there was an outcry in the Rhondda when a BBC2 fly-on-the-wall programme claimed to show life as it is in the maligned Penrhys housing estate. Despite the fact that there were credits for local residents, others protested and won the right to answer back in their own rose-filtered programme. The first programme went out on network, the reply was seen only in Wales.

The original Penrhys programme showed a depressing picture of a housing estate, where deprived odd-balls battled against their circumstances. Karl Francis, in his films, has often described the same kind of community. One of the crucial differences is that the focus of his work is in, and with, the community. The fly is not on the wall but in the midst of the action. The humour too is allowed to be self-confident and images like the laundry women carrying their black bags in African style on their heads in his film *Streetlife* help colour the depressing visual background.

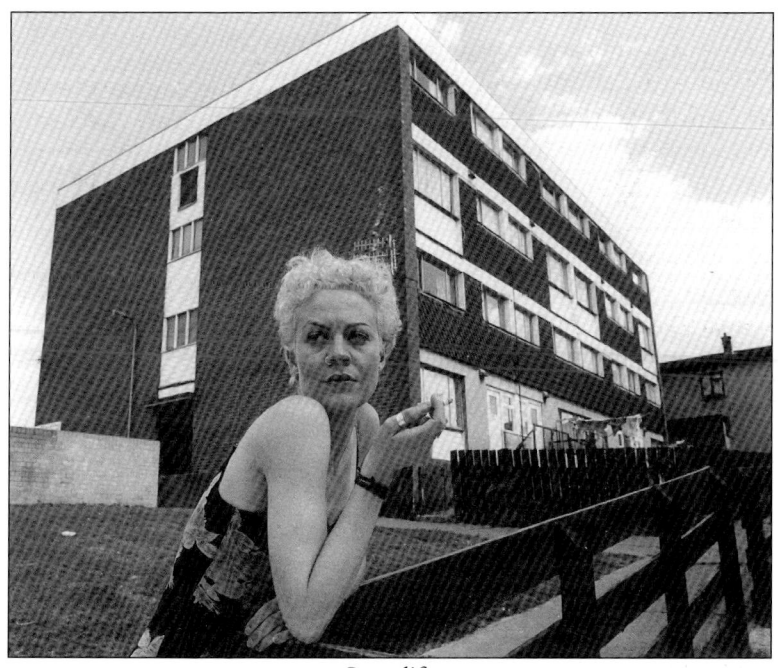

Streetlife

(Photo: BBC Wales)

One drama does not make an image. The modern media are nothing if not pervasive. While Welsh-speakers have their S4C and those who tune their aerials westward have HTV and BBC Wales, most of us still receive our images through London. The life of the imagination for many people is lived in soap-opera land, where Welsh people hardly exist. They usually flit through, and in the summer of 1996 BBC Wales was still trying to clinch the deal for a network soap from Wales.

With digital television offering the opportunity of hundreds of channels, most commentators in the field expect this to increase the pressure for more superficial and cheap broadcasting, on the one hand, and for more expensive co-production in drama. If so, it means more stereotyping, through a lack of opportunity to delve deeper, and it probably means more pressure for stories and narratives to conform to mass taste and mass expectation.

In submerged corners of the Celtic Film and Television Festival, Welsh producers and directors relate horror stories of their attempts at network commissions for Wales. 'Take it to Cornwall,' say the powers that be. 'That is more romantic.' Some ideas are refused for being too Welsh, others are rejected for not being Welsh at all and so should be made elsewhere. One may argue that the fault lies with the Welsh television industry's inability to produce the big writers and big stars, or with its over-dependence on the home market; what is hard to deny is that a problem exists and that it is important.

In his book, *Culture and Imperialism*, Edward Said spends a little time on such debates. His basic thesis is that novels and other narratives were used as weapons by the great Imperialist powers to describe and so take over their colonies. 'The power to narrate, or to block other narratives from forming and emerging is very important to culture and imperialism,' he says. The same weapon, of narrative and story-telling, was used by the emerging nations to reassert their identities.

We are back with power. Wales' image, in early cartoons or in modern television, only reflects indistinctly the country's political position and the vitality of its people. The Welsh television and film industry is where manufacturing was in the 1960s and 70s—a country of advance factories and assembly lines. Not so much *First*

Knight as One Night Stand. Marx was probably talking about Welsh television when he mentioned the means of production.

I remember one other trip. The annual Sunday School trip to Rhyl. We would spend an hour or more every year debating a possible destination—from Butlin's to Chester zoo. Invariably, the final decision was Rhyl, Gehenna of the North, with its candy floss and Marine Lake Amusement Park. It was as if the chapel elders thought we would be immune to sin if we had a slight inoculation of it on one Saturday every year.

Of the many pleasures at the Marine Lake, including, so the big boys told me, a revolving wall which made girls' skirts ride up over their knickers, was the Hall of Mirrors. I imagine Wales walking in and being stretched and squashed, warped and wilted before bumping out through the maze. Wales appears from the Image Hall, battered and bruised and eager to go through it again.

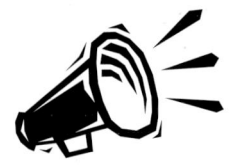

SKIDMORE SOUNDS OFF ABOUT...
AN EISTEDDFODIC TIPPLE

I was an early groupie Cymraeg. I admired everything about Wales, from its grim determination not to lose its language to its Mam-dominated family. The kindness and the friendship to strangers. Living here was like putting on a pair of warm slippers. The national admiration of scholarship removed the need to apologise for earning my living as a writer.

I have no religion myself but I admired its strength in Wales. I was given a silver pocket watch and cuff links for the part I played in the Sunday Opening Campaign but I came to regret it. I miss the peace of the traditional Welsh sabbath. Interrupted only by the Le Mans start at 11.45 a.m. as every non chapel-going male leapt into his car to be in his club at opening time.

I loved the way hypocrisies like that had been raised to an art form here: a Gothic edifice of elegant evasion. I admired the way we pretended a recent bardic tradition, invented by a druggie stonemason, had been wrapped in artificial mists of time. And grafted on to a National Poetry Festival unequalled on earth. I enjoyed the creative national urge which invented its own history.

Now I am no longer a Groupie Gymraeg. I am no Goering. When someone mentions Welsh culture I don't reach for my gun. I just wonder what happened to it. We have the language but what happened to the culture? We hold the UK record for road rage; the old people we used to cosset are now afraid to go out at night. The first act of the new councils in North Wales has been a policy of ethnic cleansing. All our children speak Welsh but they hardly have a kind word to say in it.

The National Eisteddfod defends the language but abandons another admirable tradition, teetotalism; abandoned to fill its coffers. The movement to open a drinks tent for our kids on the *Maes* provoked a public outcry. The answer. To bring it forward a year. The Eisteddfod has given a tacit approval to a private firm to run a licenced gig. It was one of the symbols of our national hypocrisy to ban drink on the *Maes* and ignore the hordes of drunken teenagers who rampaged outside. What we need now is a good old dose of hypocrisy. It made us what we are.

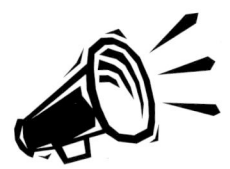

SKIDMORE SOUNDS OFF ABOUT...
A LACK OF CATS ON SUGAR BAGS.

It must be some strange perversity in the Welsh character. Perhaps in Wales beauty is only perceived through the ear and not the eye. But wherever there is a really stunning view like that over the Menai Strait at Caernarfon someone blocks it with a row of council houses. Or, worse, a supermarket. All the good things they say about supermarkets like this are true. Wide choice. Friendly staff, good products, ample car parking, sure. But the fact remains that out of town shopping places like this is doing more damage to the Welsh culture than an endless diet of Australian TV soaps.

Twenty years ago across the Strait in Brynsiencyn we had two banks, a co-op, three grocers, shops, two butchers, a post office, a newsagent, a draper, a garage, a chip shop and an ironmonger. Now all we have is a post office and one grocer. And he has to turn himself into a mini supermarket to survive.

What's wrong with that? Try cashing a cheque in a supermarket or asking them to keep an eye out for a lost cat. Do their managers serve on carnival committees, slip an extra bit of meat in the weekly parcel of families who are having a hard time? Try opening an account, chatting about the dreadful family who have moved in next door.

Worst of all imagine what the world is going to be like when the last corner shop closes down and we have to shop out of town in malls. It will be a world run by *grocers*. *Grocers* who can fix prices at whatever level they wish. Grocers who can dictate to the suppliers what we will eat. And worst of all what we will pay for it.

The day will come. The centres of Bangor, Caernarfon, indeed most North Wales towns are full of empty shops. As the shops close so the rates of the other shops go up until they too go out of business. So it's farewell to the bookshop and the toy makers. The dressmaker and the pottery shop. Goodbye to the eccentricity. To long leisurely chats leaning on the counter. And a warm hello to Musak and those perverse plastic bags that only a qualified safe cracker can get to open before your groceries tumble off the assembly line in a heap at your feet. More hygienic? I doubt it. Anyway we need germs to build up our immunity systems. Bring back the cat on the sugar bag.

Living in a Language

ELIN RHYS

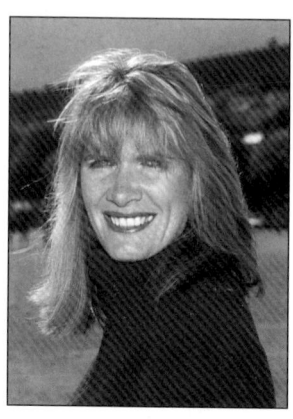

I am neither a story teller nor a poet. I observe and I feel, but I have never been able to make the string of words on the paper reflect those feelings. So here I am, in amongst the word artists, trying to hold my own. I can hear you all now. Why is she so self-deprecating, so pathetically insecure and radiating inadequacy? I have to tell you that it's partly because I'm Welsh.

I get to go about a lot. It's partly why I love the job. *Homeland* takes me to parts of Wales that other programmes never reach, and like another series I did some time ago, *Now You're Talking*, it's all about getting under the skin of real people in real places, and what has always struck me is . . . how unassuming and un-aspiring the Welsh are. Not so the incomers, mind you. They are the leaders, they constitute a large proportion of the Welsh language learners, they are the entrepreneurs, they raise their voices louder than those who have the most cause to complain. We are often more lucky than we think that they came in.

Little did I know that the very act of putting fingertips to keyboard and analysing my thoughts as I tap away would cause me to explore the depths of my own confusion regarding Welshness, the language and who I really am.

I remember being a child of the Manse, in Caernarfon in the sixties. There was no such thing as bilingual or 'Welsh medium' schools in those days as far as I knew; I can't even remember which language I used in the school yard. I'm sure Dylan Iorwerth will tell me that he and I spoke together in Welsh—we were in the same class—and I have to tell you in passing that he was the heart-throb, always top of the class, always pushing me into second place! It comes to something when my favourite memory from school is that I once earned 100% in Algebra, and he only had 90 something %! But we were great friends and even made it down to Cardiff together to represent the school on *Telewele*, a Welsh language quiz on the BBC.

To my very best friend Gaynor, the Town Clerk's daughter, I spoke in English. I don't even know if she spoke any Welsh: it didn't really matter, that's the way it was and I didn't feel ashamed of it. I even—and it's taken me a long time to admit this—took part in a school debate supporting Charles as Prince of Wales!! The majority of my class were in favour of Dafydd Iwan for that role! I lived in Caernarfon during the investiture and was offered a prize task. The honour of carrying the Bible at the ceremony was to be given to a minister's daughter from the town. I was that daughter. But that posed the first real dilemma of my life. Most of my friends, and without doubt my close family, were not supporters of the investiture. In my heart of hearts neither was I, but this was a chance to be famous for five minutes and included a visit to the Palace for a rehearsal.

Thankfully, although to my utter disappointment at the time, security at the castle meant that plans had to be changed and they withdrew the invitation to someone quite as young. It often occurs to me how I would feel now if it had all gone ahead! The irony is that, like my friends, I refused the invitation to the street party and don't consider the investiture mug as my prize possession.

But the main memory that remains from that week in 1969 is the vision of a young boy crying for his dad, in some waste ground behind the main road. I was among the first on the scene when a young innocent English tourist accidentally stepped on an explosive device timed to go off during the procession. The fact that I had looked for a tennis ball at the very same location 24 hours earlier and survived intact did not escape my thoughts. The sounds of his screams for his dad will always be with me, and the thought that he remained conscious even though he had lost limbs terrifies me. You don't remember the story in the press? No, I bet you don't; it had very little coverage on Welsh or English news, and I often wondered why.

In 1970 I moved down to the opposite end of the country. Llanelli was more in the way of being a different planet than a different town. Llanelli Girls' Grammar School was not only huge in comparison to Segontium comprehensive, you could have spent the whole day never hearing a word of Welsh if you were in the alpha classes. Being Welsh speaking, of course, you got put in the 'a' groups, inferring that you were the superior race! And let's face it, there are those reading this who think that if you were born into the Manse too, then you were made for life. So it was with this background that I advanced through school, doing all I could to avoid competing in the Urdd, and frequenting all possible junior tennis tournaments during the summer, neatly avoiding the National Eisteddfod as well. Then came the 6th form. You guessed it: most of my friends were planning on leaving for Aberystwyth University come what may, because that's where the Welsh-speaking cream go to. One science department at Aber did offer me a place there if I achieved only 2 E's at A level and I've often wondered if that was because of the nature of my mother tongue rather than any obvious great scientific potential! I plumped for Swansea University, close to the great surfing beaches of the Gower peninsula, home and the current boyfriend.

Swansea University turned me into a Nationalist. It's a great place to study and it has very few Welsh students; they are mostly from England and Arab countries. Here I had my first taste of how the English see us Welsh, studying biochemistry in a college a stone's throw from my home and yet feeling that Wales and Welshness had no part there whatsoever. All the lecturers were English through and through, and were amused that one of their students had this quirky habit of speaking in Welsh to friends and relations in Wales. In order to make a point, I did the very daft thing of carrying out instant translations during my lectures. Yes, can you believe it, a whole term's notes on respiration, photosynthesis and amino acid metabolism, jotted down in totally incomprehensible Welsh, creating terminology off the top of my head for those that didn't exist, which rendered the whole lot totally useless when it came to revision before exams. And all because I felt inadequate for being a Welsh speaker. I remember one lecturer commenting on my essays and stating how obvious it was that English was not my first tongue from the construction of my sentences.

Many years after I left university I had cause to write to him about something completely unrelated, and in his reply he said how great it was to 'here' from me! I promptly circled the mistake in red and sent it back with ... 'glad to see I had some influence'! I made no great attempts to improve my skill, haughtily assuming that having achieved an excellent O level in English language, if it was good enough for the WJEC then it should be good enough for the English who read what I write. However, the feeling of inadequacy created by my tutor's words still haunt me, and has stopped me writing many of my thoughts in English. To what extent has exactly the same happened in reverse to the people of Wales, who have been made to feel completely inadequate by superior, middle class Eisteddfod language purists?. In my opinion they are very much to blame for many people in my generation deciding not to conduct their lives through their mother tongue because they have been made to feel that their particular standard of Welsh is just not good enough.

One of the most difficult tasks at University, apart from trying to decipher my lecture notes, was being the chairperson of the Welsh society and organiser of the inter-college eisteddfod. Talk about lambs to the slaughter! There we were, a talented and enthusiastic pack of competitors up against the future framework of Welsh language media at Aber and Bangor. This is where I developed the complex that I was ... too Welsh for my own good, but not Welsh enough for anybody else's! But I was happy amongst the Chileans and the Persians who endeavoured to master the words of the 'cerdd dant', entered into the spirit of the event and at least made folk dancing appear joyful, only to be laughed at by the real Welsh! It was here I learned other things too. Like the way the Iraqis were amazed at how the Welsh didn't fight for freedom. 'But we do!' I cried in Plaid Cymru meetings that were often attended by the foreign students. 'Yes, but we mean really fight,' they replied. 'You can't have freedom without shedding blood for it.' So that's how they saw us: weak and spineless, all talk and no action, not really knowing what to fight for except that it seemed an easy option just to fight amongst ourselves instead.

College days ended with qualifications, no job and marriage. I hadn't wanted to flee too far from the nest, and hadn't had the presence of mind when choosing my subjects to consider that there were approximately zero opportunities for biochemists in Llanelli. So what about teaching, then?

I opted for a year's post grad. studies in Trinity College Carmarthen or the Trinightly College of Knowledge as it was lovingly called by some. I had Dr Alan Williams, now a labour party MP, as one of my lecturers, and Dafydd Rowlands, now Archdruid of the Gorsedd of the Bards as another. What a combination! But Trinity had a Welsh atmosphere and at least I didn't feel odd for doing what comes naturally; the lecturers had heard people speak Welsh before! When it came to my thesis, I chose the predictable title 'the teaching of science through the medium of Welsh'! My research included corresponding with many schools the length and breadth of Wales, searching for those who taught chemistry and physics in the language of heaven. But 20 years ago there was only a handful of schools who thought it appropriate to take the risk of explaining the complexities of science in a language traditionally reserved for religious studies and events of the past. Even in Welsh language schools, the sciences were taught in English. After all, there were few if any decent text books in Welsh; and how would pupils compete on an equal footing with their English counterparts at University if their studies had been encumbered because of shortfalls in the language? I considered whether there might be a market in publishing the terms I had composed during biochemistry lectures in order to start the ball rolling, but there were those far better than I ahead of the game.

My thesis outlined the lack of both opportunity and enthusiasm for science education through the medium of Welsh, but went on to demonstrate that those schools that had considered it a worthwhile venture and offered the service to the young people in their mother tongue, had been rewarded tenfold. The pupils had not suffered; on the contrary, some had gone from strength to strength, achieving places at Oxford and Cambridge. Some even managed to make it to Aberystwyth! The story is different today, even though there remains some reluctance to risk one's future studying tomorrow's science in a dying language. Terms have been created, by those who know what they are doing, and there is a framework in existence to support science education through the medium of Welsh.

My studies at Trinity demonstrated that it wasn't the pupils who faced difficulties with science in Welsh, it was the teachers. So many said to me that their Welsh just wasn't good enough to cope with conveying the intricacies of science in a language about which they obviously had a feeling of inadequacy. It was as if science graduates felt they had to obtain a degree in Welsh before talking about their subject in front of the class. There it is again! A total lack of confidence in ourselves.

I was never likely to make it as teacher. Despite reasonably good results I wanted an easier existence. During the college holidays I had been working at the local Water Authority laboratory as a technician. All I had to jot down were numbers, so language was not an issue I needed to worry about for a while. Gazing through my protective spectacles through the misted-up window, I used to contemplate the delights of being an environment inspector of some kind. You see, it was the summer of '76, and those alive in that year will recall it as being particularly glorious, and it seemed to me that the boys bringing in their samples of water from around the watercourses of Wales were getting more and more tanned by each passing day and seemed in such a happy frame of mind compared to the frazzled, fried, frantic lab workers. 'That's the job for me,' I muttered as I gazed at the bronzed water-carriers. And sure enough, after convincing myself and a few others that indeed women could just about manage to bend over bridges, dip bottles into rivers, inspect sewage treatment works without giggling, and follow the country code, I acquired the job of my dreams.

I joined a team of inspectors whose role it was to keep a watchful eye on Welsh Water Authority's own actions in maintaining water quality. This is why I feel qualified to compose the 'Good Sewage Works Guide to West Wales', and 'A History of Drinking Water Quality in Wales 1979 to 1984.' It was a great 5 years. It fed my deep interest in the countryside, made me feel that maybe I was using a modicum of my hard-earned qualification in Biochemistry, and yes . . . I won an unexpected reward: a chance to speak my mother tongue.

Often I would be found bending over a bridge wall dangling a bottle at the end of a rope. Guaranteed, a passing farmer would ask . . . 'caught anything have you?' And my well-rehearsed reply would be . . . 'no, you're the first today!' Invariably this was followed by, '*jiw, jiw, chi'n siarad Cwmrâg siwr o fod, pwy ych chi te?*' Roughly translated means . . . with an accent like that you must speak Welsh. This is the way I learnt so much about the problems that face the farming community, how incomers change communities, and how industry blots the landscape. I visited innumerable households in rural Wales to take samples from their taps in order to check the quality of their drinking water. But it was the quality of their lives that most impressed me. I listened to their problems, which invariably had little to do with tap water. It was more about the closing of schools, the disappearing post offices, the lack of transport, and the loneliness, and the sense of being forgotten. Former bosses reading this piece will now realise why it used to take me so long to return to base, but there is no doubt that it was during this period in my career that I acquired my interviewing skills.

All the pubs in rural Wales—and I stopped for lunch at tens of them—seemed to be run by incomers, as were the craft shops, and the new small cottage industries. It was the time when so many moved in from English towns and cities to Welsh small-holdings in search of a better existence. I was at once appalled and concerned about this. But how would Wales look today were it not for them? Empty cottages, run down pubs, and few entrepreneurial concerns? It is not that the Welsh are incapable of innovative ideas, or business skills. It's as though we almost expect others to do it for us, because, after all, they're so much better at it than we are!

And the times I visited households in the Valleys were among the best too; so very different from the other areas of Wales. 'You speak Welsh don't you love; I wish I did, but they never taught it round here see, and I'm too old now . . . my mother spoke it, and my father, but they thought that I wouldn't get on if they spoke to me in Welsh.'

It was about this time I developed the bee in my bonnet about place names too. Part of my job was to deliver bottles, clearly labelled, back to the lab. After a while it bothered me that all the places that I knew so well by their Welsh names, had, for the purposes of the Authority, to be referred to by their English version. San Clêr, had to be recorded as St Clears, Llanbedr Pont Steffan as Lampeter and so on. But the day I totally flipped stands out in my memory. It was all to do with acid rain, a conference which left a sour taste, and statements that left a burning mark in my memory.

Gathered together in one room in Wales were many environmental scientists from Britain in order to hear a Welsh Water Authority expert on acid rain explaining the situation in Welsh rivers. Interesting stuff, and Welsh Water, at the time, was well versed in suggesting ways of ameliorating the effects.

As the spokesman proceeded, he faltered many times over the pronunciation of some place names in the country where he, an Englishman, had chosen to work. Granted, names such as Nant Gihyrych, Afon Hydfer, and Ffynnon y Gwyddai can produce copious amounts of saliva by an unpractised tongue, and there was much sympathy for him around the room. However, all traces of sympathy from my corner disappeared when he apologised, not for his inability to pronounce the names but for their very existence! 'I'm afraid we have a bit of a problem here in Wales, with all these unpronounceable place names!' I had to be held down in my seat! This also inspired me to cast an eye over the various scientists employed in Welsh Water at that time. The heads of so many departments, and the up and coming starlets were often from outside Wales and there was only a handful of Welsh speakers. Were there no suitable Welsh applicants? Was it that science graduates in Wales didn't compare favourably with their English counterparts? Was it that they didn't apply, or was it their accent that possibly let them down?

Things have changed in the Water Industry. There is now a language policy and many of my former colleagues who are now likely to be working for the Environment Agency have attempted to learn the language that dogged so many of them.

In 1984 I left my job with Welsh Water at Llanelli to follow the flow of a different medium. S4C was born, and a Welsh language science series was required. HTV employed me to research and present a kind of Welsh *Tomorrow's World* with one tenth of the budget and one tenth of the staff. My boss was one of the few real gentlemen in the business: talented, kind, patient, long-suffering and always cheerful and mindful of other people's feelings. His name was Dewi Bebb, a former rugby international and sports journalist who sadly died early in 1996, far too young. I remember how we used to have lunch in cafes around Wales, Dewi in the corner with his pipe, sharing stories with the crew. There would always be a group of old boys in these cafes, and the excitement in the air when Dewi walked in was palpable. They would come and talk and exchange memories of past matches. Dewi was always enthusiastic and charming, even though each week, the boys, though different on each and every occasion, would always remember the same moments. I learnt a lot about humility from Dewi, who never considered himself special, although his fans worshipped him.

Cleaning up the rivers and beaches of Wales was a challenge, but was much easier than finding individuals to discuss scientific issues in Welsh on television. Some were brilliant, and the temptation to use the same ones over and over again was often overwhelming. Neither was there a shortage of Welsh speaking experts on all sorts of fascinating, televisual topics.

Indeed, it is surprising how many pioneers out there in the big wide world, who are uncovering major new finds in science speak Welsh to boot! But, persuading them to discuss it on television was harder than getting the Towy to flow uphill. '*Smo Nghymrâg i'n ddigon da ch'weld, bachan o Lanelli i fi*' roughly translated means my Welsh isn't good enough, but in reality means, 'even though I'm pretty good at what I do, and even though I do speak Welsh at home, it isn't good enough to please the so-called middle class language purists, bards and teachers and I don't want to make a fool of myself.' And besides that, there's the technical jargon. 'How do I say "neutral density filters" or "gene replication" or "immunoglobulins" in Welsh?' Sadly it doesn't help when you gently suggest that 99% of the audience won't understand the terms in English either.

But it wasn't just the scientists. All through my career, ordinary people have refused on countless occasions to take part in programmes because they feel that the particular Welsh they speak is not good enough. Afraid of an English word accidentally tripping out, and giving them away. People with wonderful stories to tell, and charming ways of telling them, afraid of using their mother tongue.

The saddest fact I faced in trying to establish a career in science broadcasting, was that there was no audience. The viewing figures were low, so low that only two series were made and no serious attempt has been made since to provide Welsh speakers with a strong science magazine series. Even a recent astronomy series with the most mind-blowing photography and computer graphics going, as good as any other series in English, was met in the Welsh language press with scepticism. The attitude prevailing was . . . why should we cultured folk be subjected to new terms, new ideas, and hair-raising concepts in Welsh? So while I bemoaned the lack of enthusiasm for taking the language into the 20th century, and the indifference of the S4C audience, and the frustration of scientists with an inferiority complex, another knock was given to my already dwindling self esteem. Let's broadcast in English instead then. Science programmes get a decent following, and if new terms arise, no one gets paranoid about them, they just get on with it, accept they don't know what they mean, find out, and then remember them. Having applied for a post in London with Welsh tongue in cheek, I was actually given a job on the grounds of my scientific background on a series for BBC 2.

Day one in a large studio in Television Centre, London. My co presenter was Martin Young who had the poshest of English accents. I placed my earpiece in my ear allowing me to hear all comments and instructions from the director's gallery and waited for my cue. There was silence and then I started to read the link I had painstakingly written and was now on the auto-cue before me. Terrified that my biochemistry tutor's words all those years ago would come back to haunt me here, I had worked hard at writing my script, but it only took them three words to burst out laughing. Yes, guffaws from the gallery, and all I had said was . . . 'There are other . . .' Instantly I apologised for whatever my mistake had been; after all, those of us brought up in a non-conformist environment have humility and, more important, guilt, ingrained in them from birth! 'Sorry, what did I do wrong?'

My crime? Rolling my Rs. In English you don't say 'there are other . . .' You say 'theh ah otheh'! I guess I should have laughed along with them, but all of a sudden I felt I didn't belong, wasn't good enough, and was reluctant to continue. It is no coincidence that Welsh accents on network television are rarer than any other accents in Britain. The tide is beginning to turn slowly, and that is due to the genius of journalists like Huw Edwards and Guto Harri, who have probably had to be outstanding in order to have their accents accepted.

But I didn't give up there. I struggled on, and was given considerable work in the schools department. My last project was teaching sex education to all 9 to 11 year olds. The fact that soon all young people in Britain will have heard about sex first by means of a Welsh accent appeals to my sense of humour. Who knows, they may even roll their Rs in 'sperm'!

But it's the lack of understanding about Wales and the Welsh language in England that really amazed me, and indeed continues to do so. I was once asked by a wonderful BBC London producer to sing along to a record that was currently in the Top Ten. A Welsh language version of this series was also in production, so I asked him which Welsh song would he like me to use. The blank stare was revealing. 'Well, the same song of course.' 'Don't be daft, why use an English pop song in a Welsh medium school? It won't go down terribly well.' 'You mean there are Welsh pop songs to be had?'

When I'd finished with him he knew all about the Welsh pop scene, was terribly enthusiastic about it, borrowed my cassettes, has never given them back, says he still listens to them in his car and keeps muttering 'why didn't I know this before?' For ages I thought it disgusting that English people, especially those involved in the media, had so little knowledge of Wales. But whose fault is it really?

Ours.

On holiday, year after year, I am asked by the various friends that we make and by people on the next table at cafes somewhere on the continent, 'Which language are you speaking?' So these days I say, 'Guess?' And they do, they try every option including Hindustani before coming to Welsh. 'You mean people actually speak it?' Shouldn't they be ashamed that they don't know about it? No, whose fault is it that they don't know? Ours.

The people on holiday with us wonder why my little girl can't hold a conversation in English. I explain the set up here in Wales. 'But won't it hold her back?' they ask. I say 'no of course not, something else will do that.'

The most rewarding time of my career was presenting a series of 72 programmes for people who wanted to learn the language. *Now You're Talking* was a huge success, and people still come up to me on the street calling me 'teach' and practising their new-found skills on me, usually when I'm in a supermarket, desperate to get home! They may well have tried and failed, they may have found it too hard or too time-consuming. But they got off their butts and tried. And if more Welsh speakers took the trouble of helping them, then maybe not so many would fall by the wayside.

And so to *Homeland*!

There has been so much talk recently about national identity and pride. Our flagging rugby side has made us dip even deeper in the doldrums, and so many worthy programmes are produced pro-claiming that Welshness is all about living in the valleys with all the angst that entails, and how we are a friendly, deeply cultured people. *Homeland* is all about digging deep into issues that affect the people of Wales, their homes and the countryside that is such a vital part of Welsh life. To that end the series works well, poses questions that need to be addressed and tries to provide answers and information to those that live in a changing Wales. But what has *Homeland* shown me? It has brought it home how fragmented we are, and how badly we need something to make us feel good about ourselves. Some would argue, as they did in the press recently, that all it takes is a hero for us to look up to, like Ryan Giggs, Anthony Hopkins, or someone to fill the gap that Burton left! But although it would help our flagging self esteem, it's not what we need. We need a good dose of 'feel good'. And it comes down to language. Words.

The greatest enemies we have are the chips that sit on so many of our insecure shoulders, preventing us from uniting in a pride in our homeland. It's not the Welsh v the English, it's the Welsh-speaking Welsh v the non-Welsh-speaking Welsh people, with both sides conveniently forgetting that whether or not we speak the language is largely an accident of birth.

But I think I've cracked it! I did something one evening in the National Eisteddfod in my home town of Llandeilo that makes me proud of myself. Mind you, the decision was not wholly mine; there was a total of three of us adjudicating the Welsh Learner of the Year competition, and we anguished, argued, analysed and learned a lot about each other over a period of eight hours on the day of the final reckoning. We came from different corners: a former learner, himself a winner of the title and man of the cloth in Blaenau Ffestiniog, John Gillibrand; a lady who has helped innumerable learners to 'cross the bridge' and has been at the forefront of many institutions that guard the language and its future, Ellen ap Gwynn, and myself, 'confused from Llanelli' with all my baggage and insecurities. There were four finalists, and each had learnt Welsh well in less than five years, in fact, most had done so, to perfection, in two!

We interviewed them in great depth, each in turn and in private, to know their views, feelings, background, and dreams for the future; the usual kind of thing. We listened to them give a speech to a packed audience, and studied them as they answered four horrifying questions at the microphone with no time to prepare before hand.

The two ladies of the four were from London originally, and had moved here to fulfil their dreams. Their Welsh was outstanding, listening to it flow was a humbling experience, as was the effortless speech of one young man from Pontypridd who now lives with his wife and new baby in Hwlffordd. Any one of these three, Sue Willis, Lynn Phillips, or David Lloyd-Thomas, would have been a safe, justified and popular choice as winner.

Number four was from Newport, Gwent. He had left school at 16, had lived in England for 20 years as a professional footballer, and played for Wales. Now I had never heard of him, and before you find that appalling, consider that football was frowned upon in Llanelli in my schooldays; there's only one kind of ball, and it ain't round!

His Welsh was not perfect, one English word accidentally slipped out when talking in front of all those people, and his mutations made mine appear like those in the Gorsedd of Bards. But he radiated enthusiasm about the future of the language, about his dream of bringing the language into sport, of training kids on pitches through the medium of Welsh. He goes around schools promoting sport and the language at the same time. Let's face it, he is the man who taught Vinny Jones to sing *Hen Wlad fy Nhadau*, and even I have heard of *him*. Now, if he can do that . . .

We took into consideration every angle in making our decision. The location and environment in which the contestants learned the language, their background, their academic abilities; one was a linguist, the other a graduate from Oxford, and the third was a very literary and cultured lady.

Marc Aizelwood is none of these. But against many odds and with frequent teasing from former team mates; from a background with almost no opportunity to practise his new-found skill he has risen to converse in a natural, down-to-earth, and inspiring way.

The language purists will frown. There will be those who feel that the honour should have been bestowed on one who had achieved perfection. We too, agonised on this point when reaching our decision.

The Welsh Learner of the Year 1996 is Marc Aizelwood. The imperfections in his tongue will speak volumes. He will inspire those who feel that they don't have it in them, that they will never be good enough to impress the middle class purists, that they will

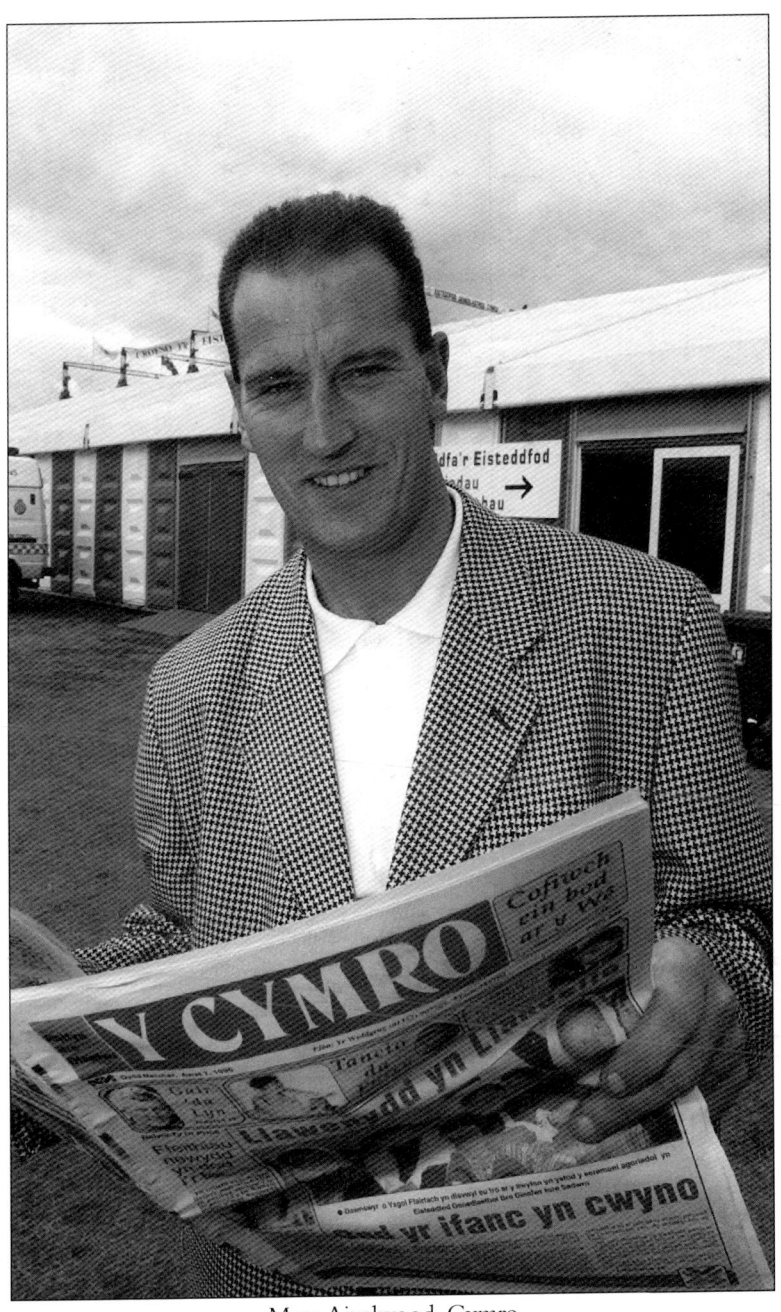

Marc Aizelwood, Cymro

(Photo: S4C)

never be truly accepted by the Welsh. There will always, thank goodness, be those like the other three who achieve remarkable goals in very little time, and will inspire others to do the same. But there won't be many more like Marc unless we break the rules, tread new ground, push forward, and say it's OK to speak Welsh, even if you make mistakes. He had the guts to come forward. We had the guts to choose him and I'm glad to have been part of the decision.

And do you know what he did in his thank-you speech? Commented on how disappointed he'd been earlier in the day to hear kids on the playing field at the National Eisteddfod being coached in English. He's shaking us up already. I rest my case. Go for it, Marc!

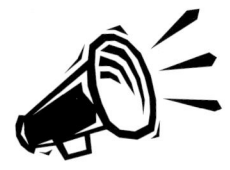

SKIDMORE SOUNDS OFF ABOUT . . . 'PHONE NUISANCES

If you had something important to say to me it is unlikely you would shout it out in a roomful of people. So it follows that what people are saying when they shout down mobile phones in pubs and railway compartments isn't important. So why are they spending up to fifty pence per minute in call time and rental, saying it?

And if the mobile phone is such an asset why are they virtually being given away everywhere you look? Not only phones either. You need a fork lift truck to carry the gifts away. The only accessory you don't get is the motor car to use it in.

A quarter of a century ago I had one of the first car phones. Brilliant reception, just so long as you were circling the mast. Out of sight you went out of your mind trying to make contact with the outside world. No problem now. It is the masts which are circling round the motorist. One of the smallest companies nevertheless reckons it will need to put up hundreds of masts in Wales. Look on the bright side. It will block the view of wind farms.

A marvellous thing technology. I once used my pioneering phone to book a table at an eating house in Tremeirchion. Started calling as we left Chester twenty miles away. By the time we got through I was driving into the pub car park . . . just as the last table went. Wouldn't happen now? It did a month ago in mid-Wales.

Marvellous century for invention, fair play. The CD Rom, Internet, the Video, the left-handed cheque book. What is marvellous is the way the lack of need can be identified and immediately filled. For most of us the Information Highway is a cul-de-sac and we see no point in going down it.

On trains in Japan, the birthplace of useless gadgetry, the use of mobile phones is only permitted in the space between carriages. Impossible in this country where that space is usually filled with passengers unable to find a seat. But what about the carriage roof? Much better reception surely? And what a relief for the rest of us.

Going Wild for Woodland

MALCOLM SMITH

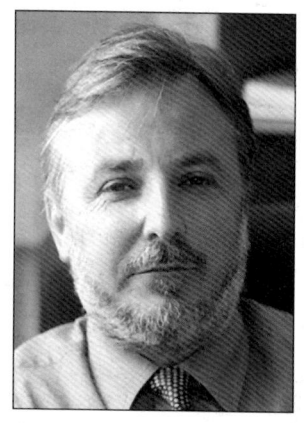

On a spring day in Bodysgallen Woods near Llandudno, it's never difficult to become convinced of the richness of broadleaved woodland for wildlife. Massive oaks and ashes tower above; thickets of shrubs including green-stemmed spindle and foamy-white flowered blackthorn impede the view; and the woodland floor is speckled white with wood anemones and pink with early purple orchid. Willow warblers and blackcaps compete in song, woodpeckers drum on hollow trunks and the dead fallen branches are alive with a myriad of beetles, springtails and spiders.

But walk a few hundred yards in any direction and it soon becomes obvious how small Bodysgallen Woods are. Surrounded by emerald green, rye grass fields where fertilisers and herbicides have kept any semblance of wild plants at bay, this isolated, few hundred acre remnant of a habitat which once clothed most of Wales is sadly typical of the demise of our richest wildlife habitat country-wide.

After the last Ice Age, most of the country—with the exception of the high mountains, the wettest marshlands and lowlying coast—was covered in woodland, mixed broadleaved forest in the lowlands; oak, birch and rowan in the uplands; alder and willow on damp ground. In Wales felling for timber, for iron smelting, clearance for farming and other development has reduced perhaps a couple of million hectares of this natural woodland to a total area of less than 31,000 hectares. Even that is scattered in a myriad of smallish fragments such as Bodysgallen.

The total area of land under trees in Wales is, of course, very much higher at around 240,000 hectares. But 170,000 hectares of this is conifer plantation—mainly using tree species like spruces and pines from North America—plus another few tens of thousands of hectares of planted broadleaved, or mixed conifer/broadleaved woodland.

But woodland is not simply any old collection of trees. Natural woods—like the hillside oakwoods of Snowdonia or the ash, beech and yew woodland of the lower Wye Valley—are home to a cornucopia of plants and animals. Planted woods, especially those comprising trees not native to Britain, can't compete. Closely planted conifers are particularly poor in comparison.

On acid soils, birch, oak and rowan often dominate our native woods, with hazel and holly in the understorey. On more rich, alkaline soils, ash often dominates with wych elm, wild cherry, hornbeam and field maple. Yew woods are the only native conifer-dominated woodland south of Scotland.

The trees themselves provide a habitat for lichens, mosses, liverworts and even some ferns to grow on. A ground layer of grasses, ferns, and flowers including, in many woods, a springtime flower show of bluebells, wood anemones and wood sorrel, is typical of most lowland woods. In the wetter west and north of Britain, a plethora of mosses, some of them rare, can carpet boulders and tree boles.

Add to this the huge number of invertebrates—from weevils and ants to bees and butterflies—and woodland birds including a plethora of warblers and tree specialists like the woodpeckers, and it isn't surprising that native broadleaved woods are our richest habitat.

According to the panel of experts appointed to advise the UK Government on biodiversity (the new eco buzz word for plant and animal species variety), 46 woodland species—mostly invertebrates and plants—have become extinct in Britain over the last century while another 78 are in rapid decline. That constitutes a greater decline than for any other habitats. But, considering that our native woodland is now a tiny remnant of what there once was, it's surprising, perhaps, that we haven't lost more.

Wales hasn't just lost woodland. It has witnessed a substantial decline in nearly all of its wildlife-rich habitats, from the heather moors of its rolling hills to the flower-rich hay meadows of the valley bottoms. Fuelled by the EC's Common Agricultural Policy (CAP), Wales' land area (80% of it is farmed) has been transformed since World War ll.

Meadows and pastures, rich in flowers and alive with insects, have been ploughed up; wetlands drained; moorlands cultivated and transformed to grassland; and crops sprayed with copious quantities of insecticides and selective herbicides. Our habitats, and the wildlife they supported, have been sacrificed at the altar of increasing food productivity irrespective of its cost in money or environmental terms.

A fifth of the moorland area in England and Wales was lost in the four decades to 1980. Much of what is left of this habitat in Wales is overgrazed by sheep, the numbers of which have increased dramatically over the same time period as the juggernaut of CAP intensive agriculture drove across the farmlands of Wales. When such moorland becomes patchy and too well nibbled, burning it can be the death knell. A habitat that nurtured bilberries, dragonflies, red grouse and impressive hen harriers can, all too easily, be transformed into a monotonous carpet of grasses, good for sheep but nothing else.

Sheep have also damaged a large proportion of what broadleaved woods remain, especially in the uplands. Not only have they grazed the plant-rich woodland floor to a billiard table-like turf, but they have also chewed off any seedling trees. In consequence, up to three quarters of the woodland area, in some parts of Wales, has, in recent years, been so heavily grazed that it had more in common with a parkland than a natural wood. Without fencing sheep out, such woods will, quite literally, die of a nasty graze because no young trees can replace those currently forming the woodland canopy.

Slowly, the tide is turning. Coed Cymru—a partnership of Countryside Council for Wales (CCW), Forest Authority, Local Authorities and the Farming Unions—has brought 7,000 hectares of broadleaved woodland back into management since it was set up in 1985. Fencing, to prevent livestock access, has been a priority but so, too, is the creation of markets for Welsh wood products—grown sustainably in Welsh woodlands—so that farmers and landowners have an incentive to care for their woods.

Well over 7000 hectares of the most typical examples, and the richest for wildlife, have been designated by CCW as Sites of Special Scientific Interest. Many are subject to management agreements between CCW and their owners in order to ensure that they are conserved and managed appropriately, both to guarantee

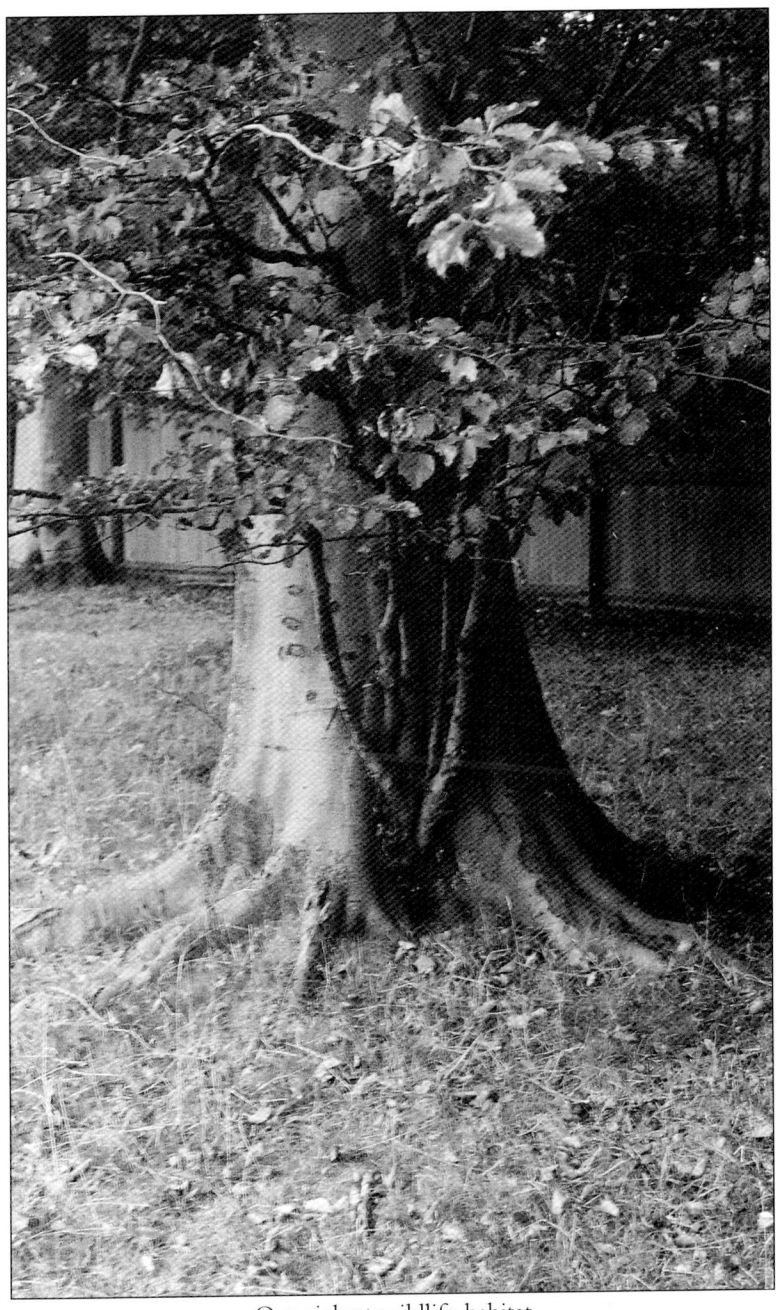

Our richest wildlife habitat

(Photo: Erica Williams)

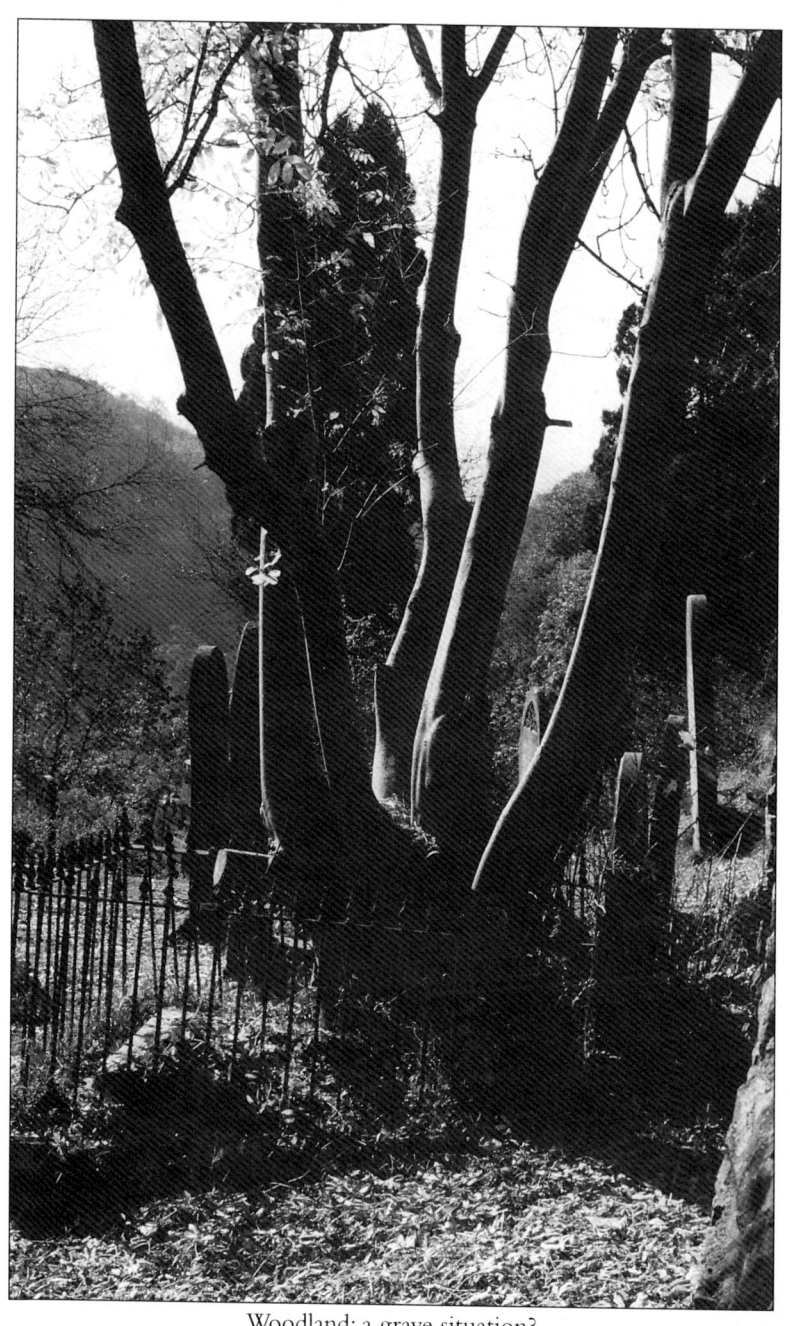

Woodland: a grave situation?

(Photo: Erica Williams)

their long term survival and to retain their plant and animal richness. Over 1,300 hectares of this SSSI area are designated as National Nature Reserves, bringing them directly under CCW's management in trust for the nation. In addition, voluntary conservation bodies including The National Trust, The Woodland Trust, The Wildlife Trusts and the RSPB own smaller areas.

The Forest Authority offers a range of grants, both for planting new broadleaved woods and for protecting and enhancing existing ones. Its emphasis has moved, over the years, away from timber production as their sole aim to multipurpose woodland use where landscape, wildlife and quiet recreation all play a major part. Increasingly, the Forest Authority is emphasising appropriate management to enhance woodland biodiversity.

Several new woods, albeit on a small scale, are being planted near towns and cities, an initiative which will, hopefully, increase public understanding and experience of the wonders a woodland has on offer. Very slowly, because planted trees may take centuries before they develop the richness of wildlife a natural forest possesses, Wales is beginning to regain some of its long lost wooded landscapes.

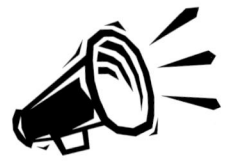

SKIDMORE SOUNDS OFF ABOUT . . . PARK PROBLEMS

If someone came into your garden and said: 'Right this is a national park and that greenhouse will have to come down.' How would you feel? Your eyes might just pop out.

Now you know how my friends the Snowdon farmers feel about that towering monument to collective absurdity, the Snowdonia National Park Authority. Snowdonia isn't a park. It doesn't have ducks on a lake, a bandstand and ice-cream carts. Well not so far it doesn't. At the moment it is a collection of small farms and businesses, WHO OWN THE LAND. It is a Community of people trying to make a living the hard way. A Community which thinks the Authority which has been put over them is more interested in hang glider pilots and climbers and walkers and people whose hobby is dog running.

In fairness the Park Authority does create jobs. Mostly for freelance journalists and newspaper columnists like me. I have even higher hopes for the new Snowdonia Park Authority which fittingly came into being on April 1. It has eighteen members in the nearly as new lavish HQ it has built, an early decision was to award themselves £50,000 a year expenses. That is five times the disposable income of a sheep farmer.

What is their job? Ask the 80 householders in Beddgelert who were told by the Park Authority that they faced prison if they did not replace their plastic window frames. Or the man who was told of course he could have an aquarium. But he must only stock it with British fish because exotic ones might attract tourists. Perhaps you had better not ask the man who wanted to put up a shed to breed ostriches commercially at Penmachno. Ostrich meat tastes like beef so he could be on to a good thing. The way things are. He had a site visit from two park officials and six members. They said an ostrich shed was fine. But not 40ft long as he wanted. Twenty five foot long was plenty for the two ostriches he was buying. Perhaps a little of the fifty thousand pounds should be spent on a book about the ostriches and the bees. The purposes of buying two expensive ostriches is to B.R.E.E.D.

They might spend a little more changing the name to the Permanently in the Dark Authority.

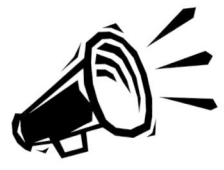

SKIDMORE SOUNDS OFF ABOUT . . . GUN LAWS

I shot a rat the other morning and I am still upset about it. I learned to shoot in a crack infantry regiment but that was the first time I have used my handgun since I bought it three years ago. So don't put me down as pro-gun. What I am pro is justice. And I am tired of legislation by sub-editor.

The right to bear arms in America was imported from this country where it was part of common law for centuries. We lost it in the twenties when firearm certificates were introduced. They were a direct response to a newspaper scare campaign about mad Bolshevik bombers. They were strengthened following a press campaign after three policeman were shot by a genuine madman; a third press campaign after the Hungerford madman's massacre brought further tightening.

The madman who slaughtered the innocents in Scotland has produced stories that make me ashamed of my trade of journalism. They will provoke further knee jerk legislation. The Police Superintendents' Association, which ought to know but seldom does, wants arms stored in armouries. Great. One ram raid and you could start World War Three.

Others want a ban on guns. A gun is an assembly of metal parts. So is a car. But as a killing machine the car is far more efficient. Why not ban cars? Even as firearms legislation stands it is already too severe. A conviction for drunkenness some years ago meant that a Conway doctor, a Bisley champion and the finest shot in Wales lost his gun license. If the police are called to a row between neighbours and one has a gun license he loses it.

It was the police who failed in Scotland, not the legislation.

Acid Drops of Rain

SIMON BAREHAM

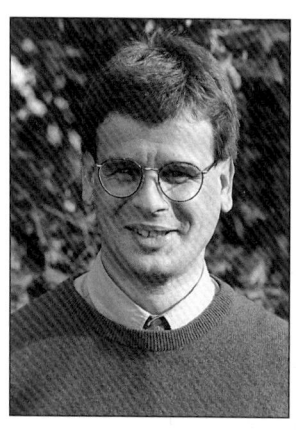

Although the choking sulphurous mists of the industrial revolution were first chronicled as long ago as 1782, only within the last two decades have the extent and nature of the environmental problems associated with acid rain been evaluated.

Rainfall is naturally slightly acidic but the additional burden of sulphur and nitrogen pollution arising from the burning of fossil fuels leads to the creation of damaging acid rain. From the industrial revolution onward the quality of urban air deteriorated until during one notorious 1952 London 'pea-souper', sulphurous pollution resulted in the deaths of 4,000 of the capital's inhabitants. Public outrage resulted in the first of the UK's clean air acts being passed in 1956. Black smoke was banned from the urban environment and power generation was ordered out of town. New power stations were built with tall chimney stacks that were thought to carry the pollution harmlessly away.

The quality of the air in urban areas improved dramatically but the tall chimneys policy had simply transferred the damage to many of our remote and pristine habitats, including much of upland Wales.

The first alarm bells began ringing when many of the Scandinavian countries reported fish deaths and declining game fisheries during the 1970s. The guilty finger was pointed at the old Central Electricity Generating Board who responded by denying the very existence of acid rain. However, it was not very long after that the problem began to sink home as rivers and lakes in the UK experienced similar problems. Rapidly declining runs of salmon and rod catches on rivers such as the Tywi gave rise to widespread concern. In 1984 the then Welsh Water Authority undertook one of the most intense investigations anywhere in the world to try and evaluate the extent and degree of acid waters in Wales. The results were dramatic—over 60% of sampled stream length had depleted invertebrate populations, mayflies for example; nearly 40% had no trout populations. As invertebrate populations declined so did the numbers of the elusive black and white dippers who rely on river invertebrates as their food source—drops of up to 80% in population numbers were recorded. As fish populations were impacted so in turn were otter populations deprived of adequate food supply.

A total of 12,000 kilometres of Welsh rivers and streams were deemed to have been damaged to the extent that they could no longer support fish populations. Such areas include the headwaters of Wales's two largest rivers, the Severn and the Wye.

Follow-up work by the Countryside Council for Wales (CCW) in 1991 showed that Wales is the most severely affected area of the UK. Over 40% of our most valued wildlife sites, recognised for their importance by designation as a Site of Special Scientific Interest (SSSI), were found to be affected by freshwater acidification.

Wales suffers greatly from the impacts of acid deposition for two main reasons. The rain that falls on Wales is no more polluted than rain falling in many areas. However, the western hills and mountains of Wales rob moisture-laden southwesterly winds resulting in a very high rainfall and consequent loading of acid pollutants. The geology comprises hard-wearing, slow-weathering rock with associated peaty, acid soils that offer very little buffering to the acid inputs. Lakes and rivers very rarely acidify as a direct consequence of rain that falls into them. It is the interaction of soil water chemistry as rainfall percolates through the soil that leads to acidification of the water body, leaching out neutralizing compounds and increasing levels of toxic aluminium to a point where they are poisonous to both wildlife and man.

In recent years a standard approach for assessing acid rain damage has been devised. The 'critical loads' approach involves the assessment of the inputs (load) of a pollutant against the tolerance of the area receiving the pollution. Where the pollution burden exceeds the capacity of the receptor to neutralize, the critical load is exceeded. At this point ecological damage to the system will start to occur. By combining information relating to soil sensitivity and measured atmospheric deposition, critical load maps can be drawn for the UK including Wales. The method has been adopted by the UK govern-

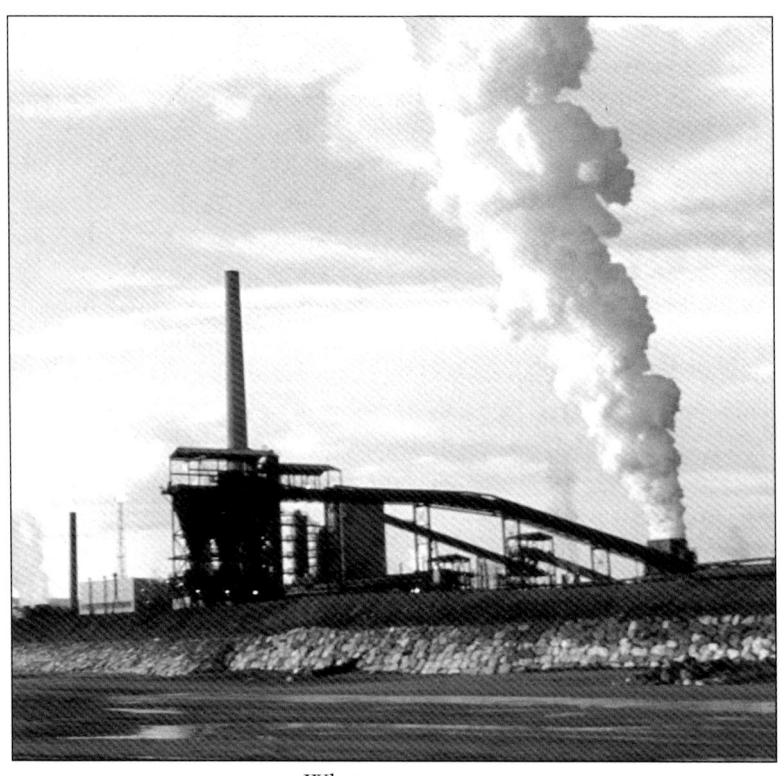

What goes up . . .

(Photo: Jeremy Moore)

ment as the scientific basis to guide policy decisions in relation to international pollution agreements.

In 1993, at the request of the Department of Environment, the UK statutory nature conservation agencies –the Countryside Council for Wales, English Nature and Scottish Natural Heritage— undertook an examination of the potential impacts of a number of strategies designed to reduce pollution. Reduction in sulphur emissions was, naturally, one of the issues to be examined in detail.

In 1994 Britain agreed to cuts in sulphur emissions of 80% (from a 1980 baseline). Even these cuts would still leave over 46,000 hectares of our most valued wildlife sites at risk from acid rain. Sensitive upland communities such as blanket bogs and their unique bog moss communities and heather-rich heathland would be most at risk in areas such as Snowdonia, the Cambrian Hill range and the

Black Mountains. On the basis of their research CCW advised that significant environmental protection would require a minimum of a 90% cut. And indeed, following collaborative programmes of research with the conservation bodies, just such a reduction was announced by Her Majesty's Inspectorate of Pollution (HMIP) in March of 1996, with power station emissions to be cut by 90% by 2001.

While this will still leave 28,000 hectares of Welsh countryside exceeding their critical load for sulphur, it is a major step forward in removing sulphur from the critical loads equation.

In the past the greatest contributor to acidification has come from sulphur dioxide, so it is good news that sulphur emissions are falling—with a 45% drop in the UK between 1970 and 1990. The bad news is that the other villain of the pollution piece, the oxides of nitrogen, are increasing and off-setting the benefits of sulphur reduction. During the period 1986-1992 rural concentration of nitrogen dioxide rose by 50% across rural Wales, largely as a result of increasing vehicle numbers.

The oxides of nitrogen have an ecological impact at two basic levels. As nitric acid it may add to the general acidification caused by sulphur and serve to offset the benefits of sulphur reductions. Nitrogen also acts as fertilizer and a growing volume of evidence points to environmental damage via this pathway. Many upland heathland communities in Wales have historically had very low inputs of nitrogen and the plant structure and communities have adapted to these conditions. In countries such as Holland major changes in plant communities have been linked to ammonia air pollution arising from agricultural intensification. Such changes may be occurring in Wales and investigations are ongoing to determine if heathland habitats are under threat from the spread of nitrogen-loving coarse grasses.

Provisional maps for nitrogen pollution in Wales paint a bleak picture with indications of widespread nitrogen pollution. The impacts and effects of nitrogen are much more complex and harder to understand than sulphur. For example nitrogen is not generally directly toxic to wildlife as is sulphur. Nitrogen is also much harder to control as it is results from most combustion processes, with cars providing the greatest contribution. Catalytic convertors can only temporarily reverse the current trend if car ownership continues to grow in line with government predictions.

Oxides of nitrogen are responsible for the re-emergence of urban smogs in cities such as London and Cardiff. During calm winter periods pollution levels exceed World Health Organization levels, leading to respiratory complaint and breathing difficulties in man. The production of nitrogen pollution within urban centres is leading to the formation of damaging ground-level ozone in many rural areas across Wales during warm, sunny periods. Ozone is a highly reactive and toxic gas, more toxic than chlorine for example, which causes damage to a wide range of receptors including trees, crops, wildlife and man. Ozone levels have been increasing across the UK at about 1-2% per year during this century. Recent work by the Department of the Environment has shown Wales to be the worst affected part of the UK, due mainly to pollution carried across Offa's Dyke, mainly from England.

So while sulphur pollution is well understood, with practical agreements to minimize its impacts in place, a new range of pollutants appear to be vying to take its place. The effects of this complex cocktail of chemical pollutants and their diverse and far-reaching impacts within Wales has yet to be fully evaluated.

The 'polluter pays' principle is enshrined in British pollution legislation. As recipients of the benefits of electricity production and with the freedom to drive a motor vehicle we all have a part to play in ensuring that the right balance is struck between the 'quality of life we expect and our responsibility to the environment.'

The rates of human-induced change manifest upon the landscape of Wales has been unprecedented in the last century. It would not be sustainable to continue at such a rate in the next century. Our most valued wildlife areas represent the last vestiges of a once undesecrated heritage. The remaining semi-natural habitats such as upland blankets bogs are the Welsh equivalents of threatened Brazilian rainforests. It is up to all of us to ensure that the remaining fragments of wilderness and the wildlife that depends on them are safeguarded for the understanding and enjoyment of future generations.

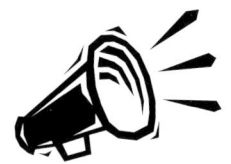

SKIDMORE SOUNDS OFF ABOUT...
FARMING THE WIND

There are twenty four wind turbines turning, and many more being constructed on the small isle of Anglesey alone. The possibility of whirring into orbit as Wales' first low flying island is alarming. Ynys Monoplane. At RAF Valley it will be a toss up which takes off first —the Hawk fighter bombers or the airfield.

The tragedy is that this monstrous regiment of revenue-for-some will be marching up and down Wales in an endless procession if it cannot be stopped. It will mean few jobs and it will be bad news for the wildlife. On Anglesey the RSPB are on record as saying it will be bad for our rare wetlands. And the flocks of winter migrant birds will be decimated. Bad news for country dwellers and tourism too. The turbines are the height of Nelson's Column and noisy with it.

Good news for landowners, *chware teg*. They will get an annual rent of two thousand pounds for each airdriven Dalek. Which you and me, the unfortunate tax-payers will be shovelling into their pockets. As we will also be financing the levy of gold coins which this demented government is desperate to hurl at the head of Manweb; boosting even further the salaries of its chairman and chief executive. Are they any good, these state of the art bird scarers? The anti wind farm group Arbed insist they are not. They claim the average cigarette lighter is a more efficient energy creator than the wind farm. It would take a wind farm covering 650 square miles to produce as much energy as a medium sized gas fired power station. The wind farm only works when the wind blows. It is, of course, an ill wind that doesn't blow someone a fortune.

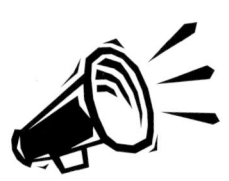

SKIDMORE SOUNDS OFF ABOUT...
WELL MEANT BAD ADVICE.

I have made it. I am 68. It's the birthday I never thought I would see. I spent the childhood in an air-raid shelter whilst Hitler rained bombs on me: worrying that onanism would send me blind. I made myself sick eating carrots because the scientists said it would help me to see in the dark.

Those were my first brushes with the nonsense scientists talk. In those days I believed them. I spent my first month in the army terrified to venture beyond the park gates. Brain washed by posters and H certificate films warning of the dangers of VD. The scientists who made them prophesied so many of us would die of social diseases it would make the Great Plague seem like a headache. In the event the only killer was boredom.

In the Sixties military scientists were forever banging on about how advanced their Russian counterparts were. Then in Afghanistan the Red Army demonstrated the difficulty it would have fighting its way out of a paper bag.

Scientists told us potatoes were bad for us. Now they hold the secret of eternal life. I gave up drink because scientists warned it would kill me. Now they tell us that prolongs life too. Fish and chips WERE bad for us. Now they are nourishing. Remember the campaign scientists waged to make us eat more eggs? 'Go To Work On An Egg' we were urged. A few years later we were told the boiled egg would wipe out Europe. The only thing that killed was the poultry industry. Remember the AIDS epidemic? If the scientists had been right I would have been here talking to myself. Now it's the beef sandwich that is the serial killer. If it moos, kill it.

It's hysteria not Brittania that rules the waves.

Life Down Under —Protecting the Marine Environment

MIKE GASH

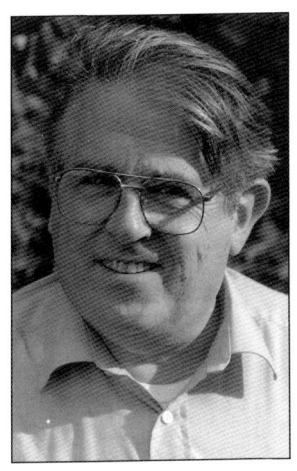

The sea around the Welsh coast is a great cauldron of life, a rich swirl of seaweeds, drifts of plankton, and fish galore. And mammals. One of Britain's two resident populations of bottle-nosed dolphins gambol in the waves of Cardigan Bay. The seas are rich. It's not that long ago that many coastal villages such as Nefyn and Aberporth owed their existence to the fishing industry. Indeed, before 1939 Milford was the principal station in Britain for landing herring.

And of course the fish support a huge range of seabirds, maybe half a million during the summer months.

Man has a landlocked view of the sea. Often when we think about seabirds we imagine them teeming on cliffs and offshore islands, in big, busy, frenetic colonies. But these are only their temporary homes. The sea is their true habitat. Anyone who has seen the return of guillemots to their nesting ledges in February will know this. Nervous to the point of neurosis they fly back to the waves at the least possible disturbance. And these are creatures of the sea. On land they are ungainly. In flight the bad aerodynamic design of their wings has them whirring frantically just to stay in the air. But underwater those stubby wings transform into superb flippers. The guillemots truly fly underwater.

Protecting the sea is a complicated matter. Nature reserves at sea are acts of imagination, lines drawn in the surf. But conservationists are coming up with radical ideas for safeguarding the sea. Mike Gash, of the Countryside Council for Wales here depicts the policies and ideas which will protect the cauldron of life.

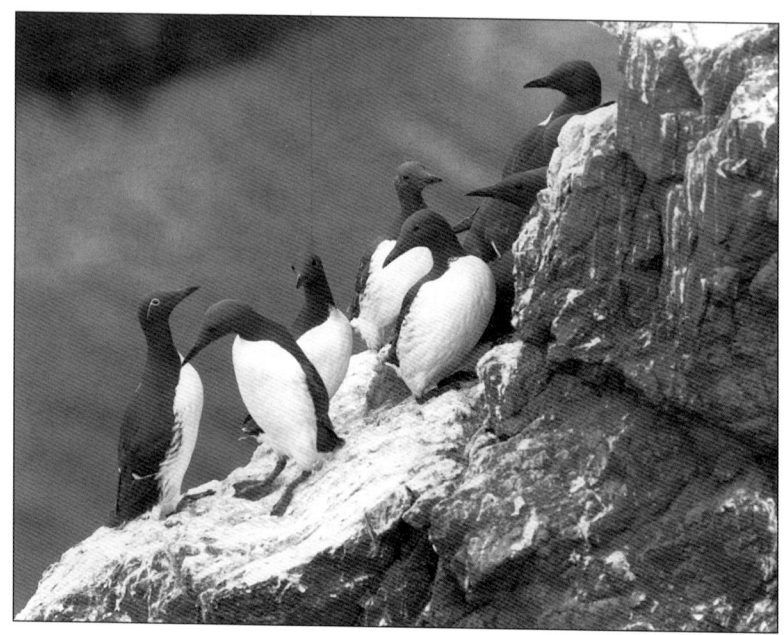

Ungainly guillemots

(Photo: RSPB)

Because we cannot normally WATCH what goes on beneath the surface of the sea, and the impacts of human activities there are therefore not visible, it was once assumed that the oceans had an infinite capacity to provide virtually limitless supplies of food, whilst at the same time absorbing all the waste, rubbish and litter that we cared to throw into them.

No such assumptions were made for the land. Here, every action and its aftermath were plain to see. Perhaps this is why a sophisticated system of checks and balances on developments on land has been evolved, (centring around the town and country planning regulations), whereas at sea there is only regulation through the actions of statutory agencies wielding certain sectional responsibilities.

Whatever comfortable assumptions were once made, it is now increasingly apparent that the seas, and their living resources, are in need of conservation at least as much as the natural resources on land. In Wales, the Countryside Council has the responsibility to advise Government on a range of countryside and conservation issues. It is CCW's intention, over the next few years, to promote vigorously the welfare of Wales' rich maritime resources and heritage. As a start, it has defined a set of clear targets, which must be met. These are: that natural, scenic beauty, the range and variety of land forms, and the abundance and diversity of wildlife of the sea and coastal lands should not decline; that the many different human uses of the sea and of coastal lands must be planned for and managed collectively, not as isolated activities having no impacts upon, or responsibilities towards each other; that there be closer communication and co-operation between all users; and that greater knowledge and understanding of the maritime zone should be achieved and widely disseminated.

These targets are beyond the reach of any one agency. The only way forward is through partnership, involving the private and public sectors, voluntary bodies, local communities, educators, and many others. CCW's role must be to provide leadership through example, advice and encouragement.

From all this, it follows that seas, shores and coastal lands must be treated as an entity, and not as separate environments as has often been the case in the past. They are often referred to collectively as the coastal zone, or maritime zone. In Wales, this zone is of particular interest and importance because of its great beauty, its relative freedom from insensitive developments, and its variety of wild life.

A tried and tested means of protecting all this, at least on land, has been through the designation of specific areas, under the provisions of various Acts of Parliament or through national and international Conventions, so that they receive special management. For example, the Pembrokeshire Coast National Park was selected for the great beauty of its coastal landscapes and for the opportunities it offered, under appropriate management, for open-air recreation. It is looked after by its own National Park Authority.

Sites of Special Scientific Interest (SSSI) are, on the other hand, selected purely as outstanding places for wildlife, geology and land-forms (or on any combination of these three). Arrangements are made by CCW with the owners and occupiers whereby the scientific importance of the sites is safeguarded. There are, at present, nearly two hundred SSSIs in the maritime zone of Wales. Some SSSIs are also designated as National Nature Reserves (NNR), in which case they are managed directly by CCW, or by a suitably qualified body by agreement. Some are in the maritime zone, including places as diverse as the rocky islands of Skomer and Ynys Enlli (Bardsey), and the sand dunes of Oxwich and Newborough.

Other long-established designations include Heritage Coast, a non-statutory label given to areas of unspoiled coast where special attention is given to public access; and Areas of Outstanding Natural Beauty, which places obligations on Local Authorities to protect against unsympathetic development.

A rather different designation is that of Marine Nature Reserve (MNR). This differs from the others because an MNR may include open sea areas within UK territorial waters. MNRs are established to conserve natural features of scientific interest, and to provide special conditions for study and research. The legislation has proved difficult to put into operation, but Wales has one MNR (out of three in the UK) in the waters around Skomer, and the procedures are well advanced for another proposed MNR in the Menai Strait.

CCW has the sole responsibility to care for MNRs in Wales. There is, however, another open-sea designation in which responsibility is shared equally between a number of statutory agencies. This designation is the Special Area of Conservation (SAC). SACs will be designated to comply with the requirements of the EC Habitats and Species Directive, which is concerned with the conservation of particular land and marine habitats and the plants and animals they support. Marine SACs will be much larger than MNRs. Environmentally friendly activities will be encouraged within their boundaries. For example, sustainable commercial fisheries will be allowed to flourish.

The protection of maritime sites may take many forms. One interesting possibility would be actually to re-create habitats which had been lost through developments, or even through natural ecological processes. For example, before the spread of myxomatosis, coastal sandy areas were often the home of huge numbers of rabbits. This was certainly the case at Newborough Warren in Anglesey, where tens of thousands of rabbits were trapped annually to supply markets for meat and for skins.

One result of this huge population was that the vegetation was constantly nibbled back, and there were extensive areas of open, mobile sand dunes, with characteristic populations of plants and invertebrate animals. With the loss of rabbits, the vegetation closed up and many sand-dune areas have evolved into dense grasslands with completely different plant and animal communities. Their ecological variety could, in many cases, be increased if some way could be found—say by mowing, or grazing with domestic farm stock—of recreating the original mobile conditions over parts of the area.

Another, more radical, example of the re-creation of habitats would include permitting the sea to return to reclaimed coastal land. Some small scale schemes are already underway in eastern England where rising sea levels allow an opportunity for re-flooding land which was marsh before flood defences were built. Maintaining such defences, where no human habitation is protected by them, is an extremely expensive option.

One of the major practical problems which has to be overcome involves the conceptual differences between conservation at sea and on land. Fences, footpaths and nature trails are established management techniques which cannot be transferred to the sea! Also, the dynamics of terrestrial ecosystems are better understood than those in and beneath the sea. For example, there is sufficient practical and theoretical knowledge to enable an oak woodland to be kept in being in perpetuity, or even to enable oak woodlands to be created from scratch in suitable locations. Such a degree of knowledge or know-how is scarcely available at sea. Another obvious problem is the lack of stable and precise (and precisely known) boundaries, as there are on land.

All seas are inter-connected, and some marine species have extremely wide ranges when compared to terrestrial counterparts. Boundaries at sea may consist of variations in salinity and temperature, or light, which can produce barriers in the horizontal as well as the vertical plane. Also, water masses are in constant motion, and land masses are not (except on a geological scale). All these factors, and many others, must be grappled with if maritime conservation is to succeed.

There is, therefore, a considerable need for research, education and interpretation at all sorts of levels. CCW intends to explore and develop new ways of communication, as well as building on established methods and techniques. If the plans for a Marine Nature Reserve on the Menai Strait come to fruition, it will present new and exciting opportunities to inform people, provide educational material, and mount important long-term monitoring and other studies into the maritime environment of Wales.

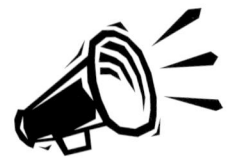

SKIDMORE SOUNDS OFF ABOUT ... CANINE MATTERS.

There was a time when a dog was a man's best friend. How come that all of a sudden he is his worst enemy? In the days when I used pubs I always took Kip, my old lurcher, with me. Now I am told there is hardly a pub left where dogs are welcome.

Why? Miss Kip is the best mannered, kindly and loyal friend I have ever had. She is fastidious to a degree I wish human beings would emulate. Yet if I take her on most beaches in Wales I face a heavy fine. Why limit it to dogs? Have you ever watched children on a beach? They can translate hamburgers and ice cream into body waste faster than the speed of light. Remember that line in Max Boyce's poem 'Barry Island'

"When I see the sea I want to pee
If I couldn't I would cry."

Shops? I suppose there might be a case for banning dogs from food shops ... though surely if they expose the food they sell they are breaking the law? But bookshops, newsagents, travel agents and dry cleaners? Where is the sense in that?

My cousin has an estate in Bath. He opens his gardens to the public and every year he adds to his entry in the National Gardens' handbook the words 'Dogs Welcome'. For years he has been the only garden owner to say that. Now there aren't ANY. This year—without asking him mind you—it was deleted. Cousin John tells me that in all the years he has been welcoming dogs he has never had a single case of bad behaviour. Children? That's different. That is probably why my favourite hotel welcomes dogs but children under the age of six are banned.

I expect that even now someone is reaching for a phone to tell me about the terrible diseases you can get from dog waste. Have you ever heard of anyone who caught the disease? I doubt it. But I can provide you with a considerable list of people who have suffered everything from paralysis to the black vomit after bathing in the sea. I would walk a dog on any crowded beach without a second thought. But if any of my grandchildren wanted to paddle in our people-polluted sea I would insist they wear gumboots and waterproof trousers. It is not dogs who are grave health risks ... it's people.

Ants In Your Pants and Other Natural Phenomena

JACK DONOVAN

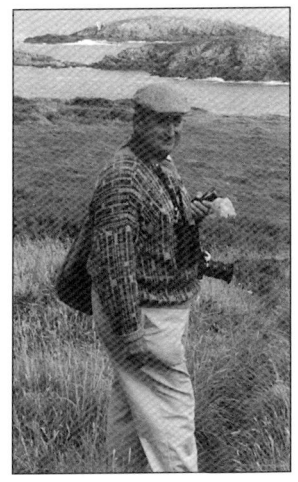

The naturalist Thoreau, who meditatively studied Walden Pond and its wildlife, would have approved of the Welsh concept of '*y filltir sgwar*', the square mile where one lives, a place you get to know most intimately. It's a square mile which sustains and comforts. Here Jack Donovan, one of the finest field naturalists in Wales, casts an eye over his patch, his native Pembrokeshire, registering the changes in wildlife which in so many ways mirror those in the rest of Wales.

A true naturalist will be interested in all groups of species—plants and invertebrates included, so it pleases me no end to express delight in the recent discovery of the black bog ant. This was a true case of 'ants in your pants' for the lucky finder actually sat on a colony and suffered as a result—sacrifice is sometimes necessary to advance natural science! The ant-colony has proved to be flourishing and one of the largest in Britain.

Wildlife has no doubt changed over the past decade, but so too have the people who are interested in and study the various groups. If you choose an obscure group for special study you can soon become a 'revered' expert and locate a first for your county or for Wales—or even for Britain and the Western Palaearctic and of course discovery is one of the serendipitous joys of a naturalist's life.

Climate change has been responsible for some of the recent influxes of certain invertebrates. The strong south to southeast winds of 1995 produced continental dragonfly species, in particular the yellow winged darter. This species was seen mating and egg-laying on the wetlands commons at St. David's and now, in 1996, it seems the species has emerged from the pupae in at least one of the locations. Of course the pool and pond enthusiasm of the last decade has been of immense help to 'Dragons and Damsels,' our dragonflies and damsellies.

I would not be too keen to see too often the invasions of defoliatory species—the effects of the pine-beauty moth in the far north are clearly made the more likely by the planting of vast tracts of land with single species of pine tree. To see the sort of damage and total tree stripping that the larvae of the brown tail moth can achieve makes me worry for our Welsh oakwoods should weather systems and climate permit the spread of species more easily.

And so to birds. Perhaps a browse through the systematic list of British birds as it is represented in Pembrokeshire will reveal interesting changes over the last decade which are reflected throughout Wales.

The black throated diver is more often seen now than in earlier years. This very rare British breeding bird, though ungainly on land, is able to swim for a quarter of a mile underwater before going up for air. Knowing what we do of the difficulties in northern breeding areas this observed change must be related to the increase in numbers and skills of birdwatchers. Great crested grebes—in Victorian days shot in their thousands to furnish plumes for Sunday hats—have attempted to breed during the past couple of years. One year they failed because of a dramatic drop in water levels in a drought year. The second attempt failed because an American mink—part of a regrettable feral population—took the eggs just before hatching. Hopefully local mink control will be implemented. The little grebe has fared very much better, for farmers' conservation pools and irrigation reservoirs (thank you, agriculture) have given the species an opportunity to expand, and they have done just that—this year a lake at Wiston has two pairs with chicks as I write.

On the cliffs that spectacular flyer, the fulmar, goes from strength to strength—ledges have been taken up that could have supported guillemots and razorbills and other species. Perhaps the well-known defence mechanism of this bird—a jet of foul smelling plumage-clogging oil is a threat to others.

Half the world's population of Manx shearwaters nest off the Welsh coast. It has been proved that these nocturnal nesters are increasing but it is difficult to assess the true extent. These burrow nesting birds are difficult to census—dangerous, indeed, to burrow, bird and man.

The decline of the tiny storm petrel is currently being investigated. On Skokholm island the lighthouse's recent change from a benign, red light to a white whirl casts perpetual (if intermittent) moonlight over their nesting terrain thus putting this vulnerable species at risk of gull or owl predation. The dazzling white tower as a collision structure already takes its toll of these house sparrow-sized seabirds.

The big cigar-shaped gannets, with their six-foot wingspans, go from strength to strength. The second largest gannetry in the world is found on Grassholm island, which lies fourteen miles off the Pembrokeshire coast. During the past decade 30,000 pairs increased to 32,000 pairs. Pelagic fish species must be available in good numbers to support such expansion—mackerel, scad and garfish feature in the gannet's diet. A recent problem has been man-made mesh and line, discarded or lost by fishermen. The birds use this as nest material and the result is hanged adults and strangulated youngsters, trapped by their own nests.

Our mute swans are doing well, no thanks to oil spills, but certainly thanks to a reduction in the use of lead weights by anglers. Those visitors the Bewick and whooper swans continue to enhance the winters. In recent years whooper swans have stayed with us in May and even into early June.

The rise of the Canada goose is presenting problems not only in the Home counties but also here in Pembrokeshire where, from the early introductions of the mid 1950s, we now have over 250 on the Cleddau river system in 1996. This delightful alien with the musical hooting call has a 'downside', for it tramples and consumes the farmers' winter cereals and grazings, it overenriches waterside areas and its aggressive nature makes it a bully when it comes to smaller, more desirable species.

The common scoter, a mollusc-feeding black sea-duck, has caused much concern because of its vulnerability to oil spills. There have been flocks of up to 25,000 between Saundersfoot and Gower, in Carmarthen Bay. In February 1996, the cruel turn of tide and wind brought a vast quantity of oil from the stricken 'Sea Empress' into the bay. We know that 5412 scoters were oiled. Such a calamity must affect breeding populations somewhere, in Scandinavia or Russia.

It is almost an outrage that red kites now breed successfully in England—east of Offa's Dyke and north of Hadrian's wall, in Scotland, I hear. Why not in Pembrokeshire? They have been seen displaying over sessile oakwoods—yes we have the habitat, and, presumably, the food supply. This is a real lament!

Birds of prey throw up a lot of questions. Will the goshawk breed? Will Montagu's harrier return? Will the increasing marsh harriers expand to breed on the marshes of the Teifi nature reserve? The peregrine has returned from the brink—only two or three pairs in the county in the 1960s to some forty pairs today. Sadly there are those who are not too pleased with the birds' return—even to the point of illicit acts against them. The kestrel, or windhover, is restricted to areas where rough herbage exists to succour the essential small mammal population needed by this predator—such as coastal rough grazing or roadside areas with tall herbs (but beware of dangers from traffic please you kestrels!) Much of treeplanting in recent years has been in rougher areas where the grassland was just right for kestrel prey. More rough corners, please!

Another lament must be the virtual disappearance of grey partridge. Hopefully this species will benefit from 'setaside' and other new agricultural prescriptions.

What happened to the coots at Bosherston pools? Could it be that that splendid muscelid, the otter, has been just too much for our coots? I well recollect watching the bow wave and head of a large dog otter by the Eight Arch Bridge there, causing all coots to leave the lake hurriedly.

Whilst the little ringed plover has arrived to breed successfully—quite recently on the extensive gravel shoals of the Tywi the ringed plover is a different story. We folk with our pets frequenting beaches—where this charming little wader breeds, snugly invisible amongst the pebbles—give the species little chance and so it is only where missiles fly and human access is limited that the birds manage to rear young.

Lapwings, curlew and snipe are unable to breed successfully now—intensive grassland systems on the one hand and overgrown, ungrazed wet commons on the other (often also the haunt of mammalian ground predators like foxes and muscelids such as stoats and weasels) rather preclude success. The past decade or so led almost to their extinction in Pembrokeshire at least. Only on the islands—where mammal predators are absent—do these birds have a chance and even there the gulls and crows take their toll of the chicks.

Green sandpipers must find Pembrokeshire much to their liking—the conservations pools and reservoirs suit them well. By July, with falling levels and exposed mud, a 'good pick and probe' is assured them.

While rare gulls such as Ring-billed gulls, Iceland and Glaucous gulls have attracted the attentions of birdwatchers, one of the big stories has been the decline in our native breeding birds, seemingly because of a decrease in food supplies. The lesser black-backed population flourished—somewhat worryingly on Skomer and Skokholm islands, then, in about 1989, breeding failure became obvious and was related to reduced availability of by-catch from the Celtic deeps fishing industry. This gull has therefore had to re-regulate its numbers to reflect the availability of food which it seems to obtain from farmed land plough following, mower and silage cutter attendance, and slurry spreading (amazing how earthworms abandon the security of their burrows and surface—where wait the gulls). This species winters increasingly, Llysyfran reservoir being a major winter roost for adults. Perhaps the young birds still venture south to Spain, Portugal and Morocco for the winter. I would!

Herring gulls have recovered from their botulism poisoning problems resulting from visits to rubbish tips. Plastic bin sacks and other developments in rubbish disposal mean that the gulls are denied their garbage-picking luncheons on the dump.

Over recent years we have been pleased to witness the increase of guillemot populations on our islands and seacliffs—the colonies raucous, noisy and ammoniacally odorous. Many of our Welsh seabird colonies are spectacles to rival those of African big game. The Sea Empress disaster has brought guillemot expansion to a standstill for the moment—we can only hope that this incident will lead to improved techniques for transporting the black stuff.

We all love the puffin, that bizarre bird with its triangular coloured bill. It seems to be holding its own—certainly a visit to the islands without them would be calamitous, especially for those hordes of youngster who excitedly ask, 'Will we see a puffin, Mum?'

Stock doves are social birds which tend to breed in loose

colonies in suitable places. They were numerous on our islands in the 60s but are hardly seen there now. Weed seed on abandoned industrial sites and on setaside areas has resulted in a resurgence of plant species. Perhaps modern rural life is 'too tidy' and does not allow too many seeding wild plants to develop to feed such species.

Of owls I lament that the barn owl is so frequently a victim of fast traffic on trunk roads and that when, inevitably, old farm buildings are improved as dwellings, nest box facilities are not automatically included.

The skylark is almost now a classic symbol of decline, in the face of an efficient, modern agricultural industry. Hopefully the new environment farming measures will arrest the decline.

Diverse habitats benefit many other bird species such as that wonderful aerobatic crow, the chough. One can also include that close cousin of the house sparrow, the tree sparrow, and while I have watched this species decline recently, it was good to locate a major block of winter stubble in the Pembrokeshire hinterland where the farming system enabled at least fifty birds to flourish.

One worries about crows such as carrion crows and magpies making inroads into certain of our nesting species—research is currently being conducted to find out whether this threat is real or imagined. Certainly in the last ten years or so large magpie roosts have been recorded and early morning drives along trunk roads will reveal many magpies cleaning up the overnight wildlife traffic victims.

Rooks are apparently stable in Pembrokeshire with some 9,000 nests. But we have recently heard about terrible onslaughts against the bird—particularly as the cereal crops ripen—when the good that the birds do cannot be too easily noted. They consume harmful invertebrate larvae like wireworms and leather jackets. It is sad that the focus is too often on the grain crop depredations. Retribution is based on an unbalanced judgment. I fear that those grim carry-overs from Victorian times, the pole traps, have been set and many a shot fired (one recent news cutting told of fields blackened with corpses). One wonders about this shooting of crows—might it inadvertently include the protected raven and chough?

In the last few years the splendid wetland system at Teifi marshes, managed by the Dyfed Wildlife Trust, has been colonised by the explosive-voiced Cetti's warbler. Small and brown, yes, but what a voice! Tarry on the old Cardi bach railway line by the Teifi and listen for it.

The recent demise of friend 'Ratty', the water vole, is very sad, but perhaps our current awareness of the decreasing population and its needs will enable those who can help to save it. River corridors and buffer zone strips will give this charming species the protective cover it needs so it can gaze with some feeling of security at the passing otter! The latter in the last few years has increased enormously and can be seen, with lots of luck, by day and night. That creature of the night, the badger, seems to go from strength to strength and south west Wales must be a stronghold area—the road deaths so often seen can only indicate a high and thriving population.

Road kill is, ironically, often a good index of the health of a given species. The hedgehog seems to feature less today in the squashed list of road casualties than ten years ago. Does this indicate a decline? The polecat was often seen dead on the roadside and sometime even glimpsed alive in a field. The past decade has seen an increase in the south west and it occurs on such distant peninsulas as Angle, Marloes or St. David's. We are finding more dormice than one thought to be present and refuge boxes for them in our more ancient woodlands are often tenanted.

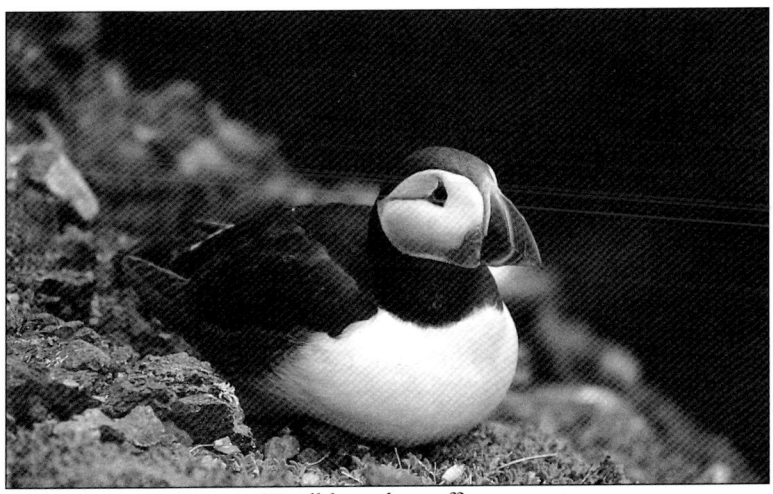

We all love the puffin . . .

(Photo: Jack Donovan)

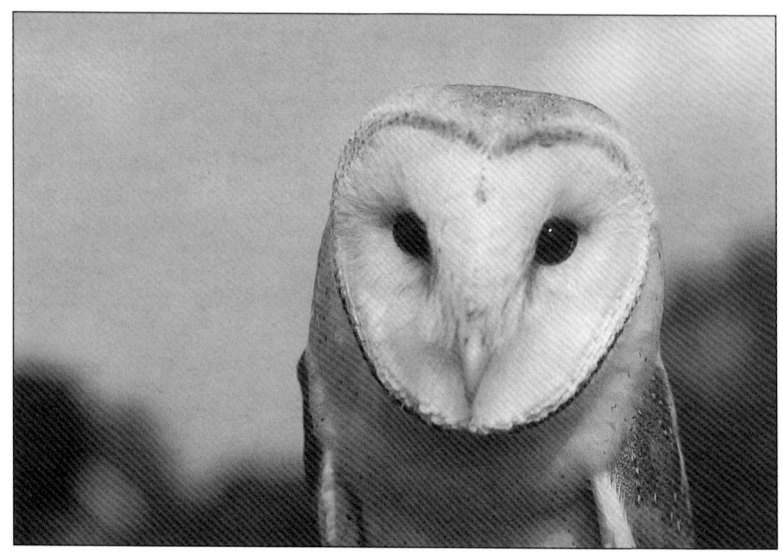

Barn Owl

(Photo: Jack Donovan)

Some groups—bats for instance—have not so much changed as that our knowledge of them has changed. We know so much more about the habits and distributions of these flying mammals, and this must be true in respect of so many discoveries.

Those wildflower meadows with interesting plant species—those splendid arable weeds of yesteryear—are to some extent returning as more people endeavour to retain and properly manage the remnant populations. Those who recreate such areas are, however rather at risk of using seed sources of the wrong provenance. I have noted many forms, for instance, of bird's foot trefoil, that clearly were not local forms and perhaps came from continental sources—or would this be worrying too much? I think not.

Certain plants have been recognised as undesirable—that Victorian garden architectural species Japanese knotweed has now been vilified—and all are exhorted to eradicate it by cutting, pulling and appropriate herbicide application. I notice though that it is much favoured by insects and that bluebells and primroses enjoy the shading canopy much as they do the similar effects of bracken. In the case of both these plants, of course, it is potentially too much of a good thing.

Certainly bracken has made great gains in the past decade but it can be said to provide the sole vertical component in some areas where birds such as whinchats and stonechats can perch as they seek their insect prey. Giant hogweed, a plant of great form and presence, is also not to be tolerated and even that attractive take-over plant, Himalayan balsam, has to be controlled. We are worried too by vast wayside patches of winter heliotrope which oust all else as they expand—but have you enjoyed the night time fragrance, one real attribute at least?

I am sorry that the idea of God's Acre has not really been taken up in wildlife terms as enthusiastically as it should been, for here the long hallowed turf is often very herb-rich, as it is too on heritage sites, and yet our need for total aseptic conditions and tidiness scatters the seeds before they are ripe. Thus, year, by year, desirable species disappear. Early purple orchids and green veined orchids are particular victims—and oh, must we remove all those ferns from old historic walls?

I have been very much alarmed to find lichens being scrubbed from an ancient tombstone—had the long interred been a naturalist I am sure he or she would have turned in the grave.

A case of real despair for me is that there has only been one probable record of red squirrel in the county this decade—we have virtually lost it while the grey goes from strength to strength as witnessed by peninsula appearances and by areas where dead and dying sycamores show the effects of their de-barking activities. The only comfort is that the alien squirrel prefers the alien sycamore species!

Yes, there has been much happening in wildlife over the past decade against a background of incomplete knowledge and personal discoveries. I think if I specialise in a new group—say stoneworts—I will make even more discoveries, certainly in terms of their distribution. For until you have a complete record of what is there you cannot too easily chronicle change.

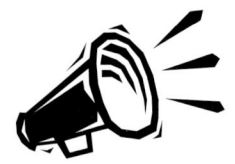

SKIDMORE SOUNDS OFF ABOUT...
VILLAGE LIFE, VILLAGE DEATH

Our village school in Brynsiencyn is a good one. Watch the children as they come out. Watch their eyes. They dance. They are alight with life. With fun, with mischief, even, if you are lucky, with the joy of learning. Watch them again, most of them, a month after they leave school. Their eyes are dead. All the light has gone out. They won't have moved far. Just to the bench at the end of the village street. There, or the car park across the road. Some will get jobs. Some will go on to university. But most of them will work spasmodically. Their real career will be standing at the corner of the street. On the giro. Too many will be on drugs and they will be stealing off their family and neighbours to buy them. Too many will appear before the courts and end up in Risley or Walton.

When I was a kid I worked in the hay. Had I wanted to I could have got a full time job on the farm. I would have been taught hedging and ditching, animal husbandry and a thousand other skills. Nowadays we don't even bother to keep them down on the farm. We have got machines that do the work of ten. JCBs, their metal necks stretched like pterodactyls, chase each other round our country lanes in absurd mock mating rituals. There will be no jobs for the not so bright village children. Their future is already over. The rot set in with the little Fergie tractor. Now if there is a farm job there is a machine that can do it. What for? Efficiency. What is the result of this efficiency? Butter mountains. Wine lakes. Farmers pouring milk down the drain because they have exceeded their quotas.

Half the world's still starving, mind you. Because the bureaucrats who are the real farmers haven't the wit to move food mountains. And children on street corners. With dead eyes. Frankly if that is the brave new world you can keep it. Has it ever occurred to you the Luddites might have been right when they smashed the first machine?

I prefer the country as it was. When the light in your eyes didn't die until you did.

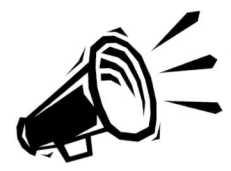

SKIDMORE SOUNDS OFF ABOUT...
TELE-VILLAGE LIFE

There are ninety televillages emerging in Wales; 38 telecottages already exist. Liberated from the kitchen sink, cut free from the cooker. Where is mum's place in the home now? Next door in the living room. Hunched over a keyboard. Some dash for freedom.

I blame the Sixties which were not only responsible for more bores than the Gun Barrel Proofing Act: its wilting flower children ushered in the dreadful dawn of denim; introduced the adenoid as a musical instrument and elevated self-indulgence into an art form. Dropping out became fashionable. You couldn't move in the countryside without treading on some long-haired oaf, untidily doing his own thing behind every blade of grass.

The telecottage is the dreadful outcome. The first generation in history to reject precedent as a teaching aid, the Sixties child ignored the lessons its parents learned. If you work at home the pay is worse, the work is harder and there is no-one around to complain to. The only good thing to come out of working in a garret was 'La Boheme.' And look what happened to poor little Mimi of the frozen fingers. Dead before the final curtain. Sewing like she did until your eyes came out like chapel hat pegs might be a thing of the past. But there is not a lot of difference between spending your life hunched over a sewing machine or a computer keyboard. You just get different illnesses.

There are sitting rooms in Scotland now that are out-stations for British Telecom directory inquiries. A question of time before they spread to Wales. You can publish a book, design a car accessory, run a TV programme ... All without leaving your front room. Big deal. Leaving your front room was one of the few pleasures the Industrial Revolution brought. Who benefits from this dreadful development? Employers certainly. No office rents or running costs; no pensions or sick pay; no holiday rosters and certainly no industrial action. Families too. As any home bound writer will tell you. So far as the family is concerned, the sitting position is the listening position; and if mum is in the house she is available for kitchen duty.

The European Union is terribly keen on telecottaging; which is probably the single most damning thing you can say against it. It has just spent £660,000 on a project in which the University of Swansea was involved analysing the effects of working at home. A cheaper way would have been to suggest to our Euro MPs they should work from home via television conference links. That'll be the day ...

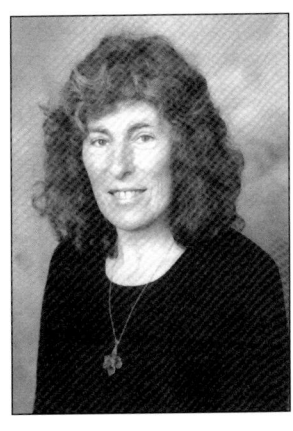

Village Voices

Am I my neighbour's keeper?

NORAGH JONES

I'm not your neighbour. I'm the person who lives in the house next to yours', said one 'neighbour' to another, after a tiff over the making of a *Homeland* programme in her community. In another community it was neighbourly rivalry over who got ON the telly and who did NOT get on the telly, that caused a tiff. Alas, how fragile is neighbourliness become in today's fragmented rural communities, when the dwellers therein cannot serenely place in context a media portrayal of their community, and weigh it against the solid everyday reflections of self-identity in their WI and *Merched y Wawr*, in the *papurau bro* and in the local gossip networks. But there's the rub. The gossip networks in fragmented communities are insulated from each other to a greater or lesser degree, whereas a telly programme is unilinear. There is the risk of people being caught off guard, and asked to talk more openly about things they usually only talk about when among 'our own kind'.

Being a good neighbour is clearly easier said than done, and country neighbours are no exception. In the luck of the draw neighbours can be the cause of long drawn out misery and helpless anger, or they can turn out to be the steady source of warmth and support we hear about in D. J. Williams' *Yr Hen Dŷ Fferm* and other eulogies of the traditional community. The clash of life styles in the countryside these days is epic. Equally epic are the 'bad neighbour' stories that circulate in such abundance in rural Wales. The moving of boundary fences has been commonplace since the middle ages, and continues with unabating verve. Residents shop their neighbours to planners and environmental health officers when driven to the end of their tether by finding their tranquil rural home threatened by the noisy hell of quarrying (licit or illicit) or old banger races.

Some are born NIMBYS, others are made NIMBYS. (Not in My Back Yard). All it takes to turn your average tolerant countrydweller into a NIMBY is to have the finger of God point to your little bit of Eden, and ordain for that unblemished plot a wind farm or gravel pit, a rubbish tip, a 4 X 4 challenge circuit—or noisome neighhours.

The trouble with the countryside is that it has to be so many things to so many kinds of people. The clash of cultures is deafening, and I'm not just talking about Welsh language and English language cultures, or about local and incomer cultures. I'm talking about the equally powerful clashes between the 'peace and quiet' lobby and the noisy sports lobby; between the 'bungalow in every field for retired farmers' brigade' and the 'stop building over the open countryside' line taken by planning officers (with little effect in the face of local community pressures). On one side you have the *Parch at Gymru* (Respect for Welsh language culture) movement and respect for the natural environment (including Tir Cymen, Dyfed Wildlife Trust and Cymdeithas Edward Llwyd). On the other you have the concept of the country as a big empty space for kicking up a racket, dumping rubbish, and clearing off at the end of the day without shutting gates or taking your litter home. Every known red kite breeding pair in mid Wales has to be guarded against the depredations of international egg collectors and the poison put down by farmers who want rid of predators, whether red kites or anything else, who might take a new born lamb. The countryside is increasingly a battleground where conflicting interests slog it out—and that's before we even get down to the clash of neighbours and the comfort (or discomfort) of strangers.

I'm a self-confessed NIMBY now, though once I rather looked down on environmentalists who only wanted to keep the countryside 'beautiful' like the Snowdonia National Park. I remember talking to a farmer in Snowdonia who was full of indignation at the way the land of his birth has been turned into a convenience for visitors rather than for the people who were trying to earn their living from it:

> The neighbours have more sense than to walk anywhere. They have their Landrovers for driving the sheep. But the old paths between neighbouring farms or down to the village are now designated for strangers to come walking by for no good reason. And the Park officers have a lot to answer for, since they are the ones responsible for this mad increase in walking

> the old paths, just when the farming community had gratefully given them up . . . I'll tell you another thing. Do you see that new bridge they are making down there? They sent a man from the council to measure it up. The river's so narrow down there that when they put in the concrete piers it will overflow and flood the surrounding land. I could have told them, but they don't listen. They do it all in their offices on bits of paper and don't look at the real thing till they make a pig's foot of it.

The nut-brown eyes narrowed in his weather-tanned face, and he spat carefully. 'An Englishman he is, that man from the council.' His brother, who had joined us by now, looked at him for a moment and then added with conviction: 'But an Englishman is better than a man from Cardiff.'

For communities in the national parks the nuisance potential of neighbours clearly pales into insignificance when measured against the menace of officials and the large scale invasion of determined leisure seekers:

> Twenty four from the Isle of Wight came down the edge of the forestry there on my land, and you can imagine twenty four crossing my fences one after another—destroy them, they do, the buggers—and that was after the footpath diversion was agreed with the Park officers, and the stiles put in, plain to see, but not to that lot. If I had my way I'd take a . . . [he struggled to find the right word from old telly films in English he had watched] . . . an AUTOMATIC to them.

Nimbyism is widespread in the Snowdonia National Park, and it is another bone of contention with the farming community that well-off incomers buy up redundant farmhouses and try to turn the countryside into a museum. I'm not, I hope, that kind of NIMBY. The everyday work of farming and forestry is fine with me, even when the hills are alive with the sound of chain saws. It's productive, after all, and seasonal. What turned me into a NIMBY was the excruciating whine of teenage bikers doing a few hundred laps round a neighbouring field every weekend. Complaining about noise is something you have to do, but it's often futile, because noise is now a way of life for so many people. Complaining just ends up reducing you to 'non-neighbour' status, even when you are still struggling to hang onto the old-fashioned belief that the people who live in the house next to yours are your neighbours.

It is not surprising then that country solicitors are all moving into plush new double-glazed offices in repro-Georgian style. Because in rural Wales solicitors' letters fly thick and fast over boundary disputes, fishing rights, water supplies and noise nuisance. Neighbours refuse wayleave for electricity to cross their land to provide power for new residents, on the simple grounds that it is their legal right to refuse. It doesn't occur to them that none of us would have any electricity if it hadn't crossed our neighbours' land. Any appeal to community feeling or neighbourliness leaves these 'neighbours' unmoved, for we moderns are far readier to claim our individual rights than to face up to mutual obligations with the people who share our *bro*, our *cynefin*, our beloved place. Mind you, even while we go for our legal rights, we bewail in the next breath the loss of community feeling and the old spirit of cooperation. It is the same mentality that bemoans the demise of the village shop, while rushing to shop till we drop in the new out-of-town Safeways.

Is there still neighbourly community in rural Wales? It is alive and well, but only if you are lucky enough to have a friendly guide, good neighbours, to lead you through the cultural labyrinth. Because there is a baffling variety of folks living in the countryside these days—farmers and townees, locals and incomers, Welsh speakers and English speakers, New Age and straight, Christians and pagans. And the division is not always predictable. You come across Welsh speaking incomers, indigenous white witches, shepherd poets, Welsh language and English language surfers on the Internet. Enchantment happens where two worlds meet, says ancient Welsh myth, and the point of enrichment is still the empathic meeting of different cultures, and not the trench warfare mentality.

The problem is that crossing cultures is never straightforward. I know an incomer in mid-Wales who occasionally has visions of an angel with flaming sword appointed by a Welsh-speaking God (or his delegates on the community council) to keep non-locals from sharing the local Eden. And some locals might well ask what's wrong with that, if it's the only way of saving the language and culture in the heartlands? A *Cymraes* from Bethesda told me:

> It's the pushier incomers, the ones who go for the plusher parts of the Snowdonia National Park, who are the problem. Around Bethesda they're younger and more hippy (though not real hippies), and they

don't interfere so much in the community, so they're not as threatening as the ones who move in and try to take things over. The worst are the ones who want to run everything in a loud-mouthed pushy sort of way, as if they had all the answers and were doing us locals a favour. That stirs things up and provokes the *Cymry Cymraeg* to more extreme bitterness about 'white settlers' trying to join in and turning everything from Welsh to English in local clubs and meetings. I've spent a lot of time working for Cadno (the Welsh language CND) and monitoring firms moving into north Wales. I'm completely behind green policies for this country, fighting rural pollution, but they have to be connected up with our way of life here and not just stuck on by outsiders who haven't bothered to try and understand what's here already and what people feel about it. What's the good of caring for the environment if you don't include the local people as part of the environment? In the Snowdonia National Park Welsh people are a threatened species too.

Fair comment, but the problem on many community councils is that they never get onto these big issues of environmental pollution or encouraging rural businesses. They get stuck on whether to have an extra street light or two, and they are naturally reluctant to expose to newcomers hidden agendas like how the intricate tapestry of local ownership may affect planning recommendations. A good community councillor, after all, looks after his or her own. Who then looks after the Others? Who, indeed, are the Others? Maybe the way we label people 'locals' and 'incomers' adds to the problems of divided communities. In my own Good Neighbour stakes it is not where you come from that counts, or what language you speak, or whether you're hippy or straight. More important by far is whether you care about your *bro*, have respect for the place you inhabit. That includes wanting to know about your place and its people, past and present; and wanting to be part of its future. A south Wales woman who has recently moved to an idyllic farmhouse in Snowdonia is only too aware of the heavy weight of cultural challenges facing her:

> Being culturally at home is important here. There are people in the village who have lived here all their life, and there's not a lot of incomers who impose themselves on local life, with their outside views which don't connect with the locals' way of seeing things . . . Around

here there aren't two clear separate communities of incomers and locals like the village I lived in before, and I feel there's more of a community feeling. I also feel that as a Welsh person from Cardiff who has learnt Welsh I have more cred here, rather than that giving me a sense of separation as it did among incomers in my last village . . . Living in a national park, though, is in a way a problem for me. It's a problem of escapism, being part of a protected landscape where incomers and townees are more possessive and protective than the locals who make their living here. But you can't falsify your own wider concerns about countryside issues, or pretend to see them the same way as the locals when you don't. Dafydd the local farmer is on the community council and is not keen on access rights for walkers and so on. His land is going into Tir Cymen and they're going to put up stiles to improve access. He's worried about people breaking their legs on stiles and suing him for damages. There's a hearing coming up on the community council because a local landowner has closed a right of way. Dafydd would be sympathetic to that (if he could get away with it). So he wouldn't represent our views, though he is our community councillor. You could get involved, maybe stand for the community council. But I feel hesitant because coming into a community with ideas from one's own intellectual background is a problem. How far do you want to start exercising your wider ideas? If you don't you're not transferring your ideas into general use. If you do you're imposing something of value, but which is alien to local thinking and turns people against incomers who fling their weight about, but haven't got roots or permanent attachments to the area. It's a question of how you do it . . .

Neighbourliness has always thriven best through practical everyday courtesies like shopping for someone, listening to their troubles, feeding chickens or cats over holidays. It is knowing you can ring somebody up to check on a local powercut or, once, a madman camping out in a platelayer's hut on the *lein fach,* our narrow gauge railway. A neighbour is someone who doesn't mind turning out to help when I (one of the 90% of countrydwellers not earning my living from agriculture) find an injured sheep who has strayed onto our land. A neighbour is someone who tells you the local stories. These are an essential antidote to sentimental fantasies both about *y werin bobl* (the indigenous good folk) and the *mewnfudwyr* (the English incomers—wearers of horns and tails or bearers of civilized

values?) It's impossible to idealise the rural life when you hear the seasonal round of neighbourly hassles—and it's a hard thing to run down rural community life while you can still give and receive real neighbourly help.

But in the long run it has to be faced that neighbourliness is wearing thin on the ground. Even farming families are far more independent that they used to be in the days of mutual reliance on neighbours' help for the hay and the tatties and the sheep shearing. There is a townee element who seem to have moved into the countryside to get more space for (and fewer neighbours to complain about) their noisy leisure activities. Their teenage offspring appear to understand the word 'neighbours' only in the context of yelling 'Fucking neighbours' at co-residents who have the nerve to ask them to turn down their ghettoblasters.

When your neighbours are not too much with you, they may be too little with you. As we lead more privatised lives, in country as well as town, loneliness is a real problem for the rapidly increasing number of people living on their own. The car culture insulates us from those chance encounters along the road that used to keep people in touch with each other on a daily basis. It's surprising how few people walk anymore in the country, unless they are 'Ramblers'—and those attract uncomprehending derision from many Landrover-bound farmers. The phone is the lonely person's substitute for neighbours, but it is a very selective instrument which rules out the pleasures of chance meetings and chats. One old lady put it like this:

> In those days people used to call when passing the house. They walked for miles on different messages around the countryside, and they would just knock at the door and call in. Now you don't get that friendliness. Everybody has cars and telephones, so they drive past, or pick up the phone for few words, but it's not the same. There used to be a very friendly atmosphere, and people calling in with the news. Of course you got the kettle on and and gave them a cup of tea, and they really appreciated that because they had walked miles from the shop . . .

In the traditional rural community residents did not need to be told how to keep an eye on their neighbours' comings and goings. The gossip so gathered was essential input to the ongoing village

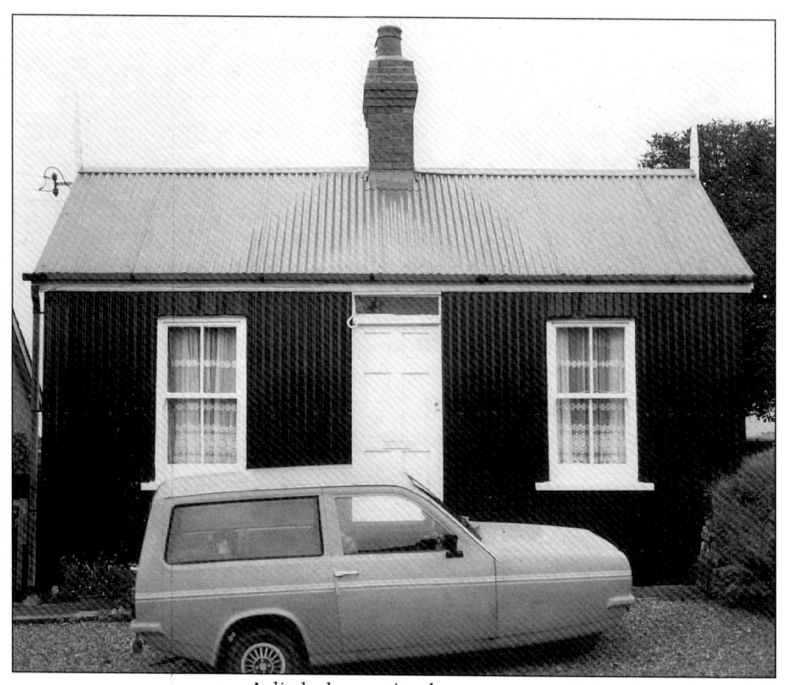

A little house in the country

(Photo: Michael Guest)

story, a way for the inhabitants to define themselves in their own terms. But in today's fragmented communities gossip too is fragmented. The same story is differently told among different groups, and there is no consensus of judgment. As the fanatical interest in neighbours' doings fades Dyfed-Powys Police find it necessary to revive it for the sake of reducing rural crime. They are currently encouraging a return to some kind of neighbourliness with their Home Watch scheme. 'Just consider,' they urge, 'how much more confident you would feel if you knew that you and your neighbours were looking after each other's homes throughout the year. Going to work, going to the shops, out for an evening or away for the weekend—you would always be able to enjoy the sense of security and peace of mind because a Home Watch scheme operates in your area! Great idea—pity it's not always passing strangers, but sometimes the neighbours themselves who are the problem, leaving field gates open for animals to stray, letting their dogs loose in lambing time ('He's only chasing after them, he's not doing them any harm'), or helping themselves to odds and ends that just happen to be lying about the countryside:

> I've just found that about 30 metres of alkathene pipe is missing. Writing things off to - - - is becoming an almost weekly occurrence. A woman on her own, busy with kids, is bound to be a victim, I suppose, as perhaps is an old person. It may be a chance to practise putting up with things, but it's not strengthening for me, and it's not good for - - -, either, to get away with it. But I don't know what to do, because I can't prove anything. I think the problem is going to get worse. I'm afraid of him and I find his behaviour threatening, even when he's not poking about the place when I'm away, as I know he does.

'Better than a cardboard box on the city streets': A Traveller's Tale

Paul is a New Age Traveller who travels around on his own in an old caravan. This is unusual these days when travellers are feeling persecuted and gather in convoys for mutual support and protection. Since the 1994 Criminal Justice Act the tendency is to clear off to the more hospitable atmosphere of hippy communes in southern France and Spain, but Paul is more at home in rural Wales, where he has lived on and off for twenty years, sometimes sharing an old cottage and sometimes on the road in his van. This is his story:

> I was living in Nottingham five years ago and problems were building up. I was in a relationship which was breaking up, and I couldn't afford a place of my own. I got a letter from a friend in Wales saying come and visit, and I did. This is where I've been ever since, moving around. It's better than a cardboard box on the city streets. Councils would rather spend money evicting travellers than providing them with sites, and straight caravan parks are too pricey for me, even if I could get along with the people ...
> What am I looking for in my travels? I'm looking for myself and everything else. I mean I do visual meditation. I haven't got very far on my own, except sometimes when I feel in touch with things. Sometimes I have this feeling of rightness about things, you know? There are moments of certainty when you can feel—no mistake—in touch with the universal archetypes. Yeah, I'm into Jungian archetypes.

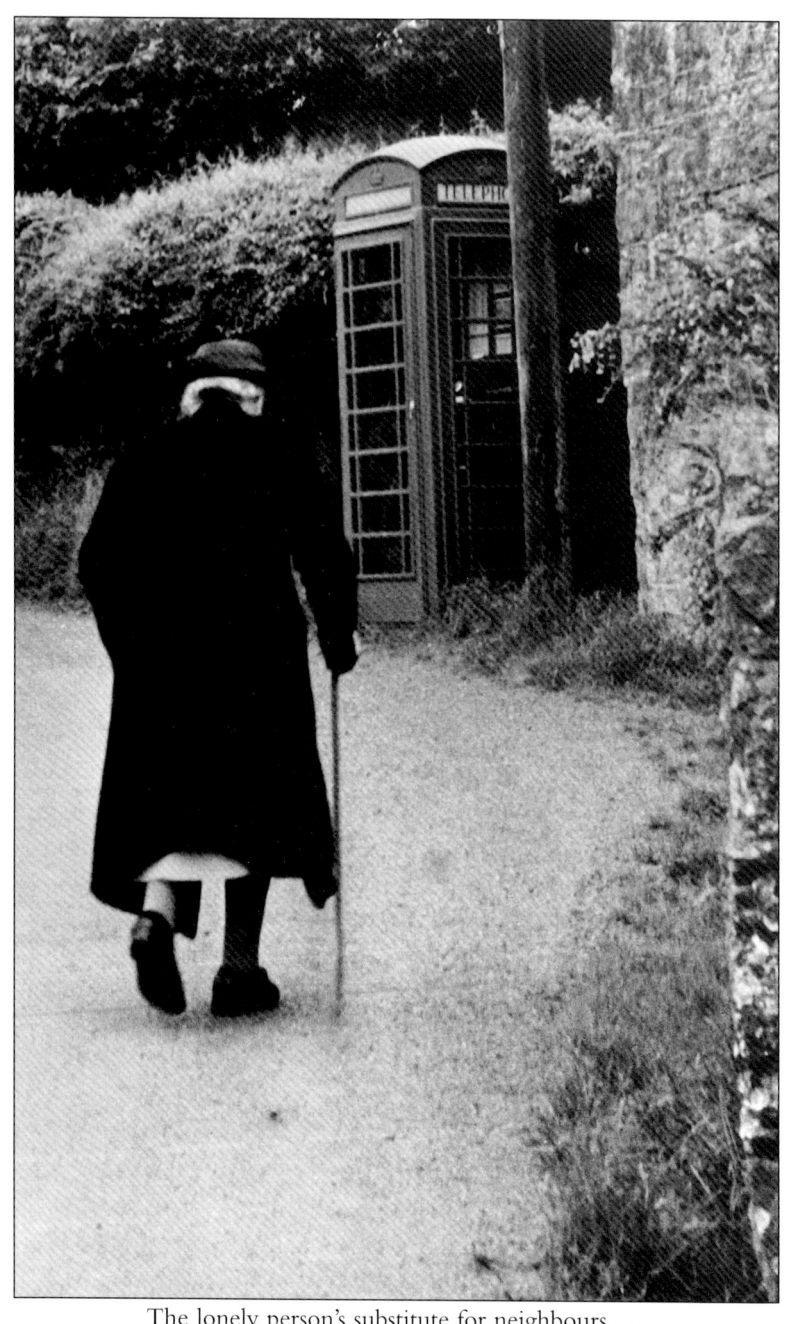

The lonely person's substitute for neighbours ...
(Photo: Michael Guest)

It's the Big Consciousness I'm after, though I don't often make it. The times I do make it? Well, I just am, and everything else is, and that's all there is to it. That's what it's like. Other times I don't get it. I'm working too much on my own. I'm meditating the best I can. There's astrology too, not the pop bit about horoscopes, but the way your moment of birth gives you a blueprint for how you can grow and what you can be. It's to do with getting in touch with your spirit guide. I've got my spirit guide, my animal spirit that I ask for guidance. When you do that things come to you that you could never think of for yourself—if thinking was all there was to it—but it isn't. There's something came up in my meditation the other day, about me planting trees, as if I were going to get work doing that next. Maybe that's the next thing—to get into planting trees. Your spirit guide tells you the right moves to make in your life —what to do and what not to do.

Paul has a flourishing rowan tree in a little tub which he puts outside the door of his van every time he parks up. It's part of the ritual of arrival in a new place, because it blesses the locality and protects against bad spirits. 'I carry that little tree around with me everywhere, because somebody gave it to me the night my daughter was born. I'm not with my daughter any more, but I've kept that tree with me ever since. It gives out good spirits.'

I tell him, 'Yes, the old folk around here used to plant rowan trees nearby their houses and byres to keep people and animals from harm. It's one of the Celtic sacred trees.'

Jobs for the Locals

Commentators on the rural scene usually point to a split between locals and incomers over the big environmental questions. 'Carry on spraying the organophosphates and bugger the wildlife. We've got to make a living', say the struggling farmers. 'Protect bio-diversity', say the environmentalists. 'Bring back the corncrake and the disappearing moorland birds. Stop overgrazing on the uplands. Stop the gravel pits. Stop planting conifers and start planting native trees.' Estate agents' brochures for selling woodland walk a tightrope between profit and conservation objectives. 'The fringe of red oak along the riverside . . . regularly stuns autumn visitors with its colourful scarlet splash. This quiet place of mixed woodland contrasts beautifully with the more productive plot ... We consider that up to 50% of the productive area could be thinned and managed for sawlog production, yielding immediately tax free income ...' And doesn't felling woodland mean jobs for the locals, too? A local woodland expert told me:

> The jobs would only last about ten minutes, and they don't necessarily go to local men anyway. The felling goes to a travelling subcontractor who works with a mate (on less than minimum wages). By the time he's maintained his machines and lost time due to lakes of mud and killing gradients, he's lucky if he has enough profit left over to pay his mortgage ... Great fellows though ... There's Effing Dave who can take out an acre of spruce before lunch, and still have the energy to prop up forked timber torsos along the track with joke placards nailed over the crotch—NOTHING TO HIDE or MR RIG or WHERE'S MY FIGLEAF?

The farming community is regularly advised to augment their meagre incomes doing B & B for summer visitors For many farmers' wives it provides welcome sociability as well as extra income. But some hill farmers are sceptical. 'We're supposed to be diversifying into tourism next, no matter if you have a remote place like this, and the weather coming over it in waves that would keep the townees shivering in their beds at night, and longing to get back to their pubs and discos.'

Tourism is a big earner It certainly provides jobs for the locals even if they are poorly paid and seasonal. But there's always a niggling doubt about what it's doing to the language and culture. The S4C evening news on 27 June 1996 announced the planning go ahead for a big holiday village at Morfa Bychan near Portmadoc. The locals were divided. '*Mwy o bres i'r ardal am dwristiaeth*' ('more money for the locality from tourism'), said the 'Jobs for the Locals' school of thinking. But Councillor Dafydd Iwan pointed out the impact on the identity of the area. 'It's out of balance', he said. Local protestors were parading with placards saying *Cadwch Morfa'n fychan* ('Keep Morfa small'), but an equally local caravan park owner not surprisingly came out for development. The bottom line is 'Jobs for the locals', even in the language heartlands.

The irony is that for Welsh speaking youth in 1996 there are Welsh language tourism jobs in Walt Disney World, Orlando, Florida, but not necessarily in their native locality. Walt Disney World advertised in the *Cambrian News* for young Welsh speakers to work in Magic of Wales/*Hud Cymru* in Florida, and be trained as Walt Disney managers. Meanwhile, back home in Pembrokeshire, there are jobs for the locals (but not Welsh speaking) as fun operatives at the Oakwood theme park, which offers its own version of Welsh heritage:

> EIGHT MILES OF RIDES 80 ACRES OF FUN . . . Megafobia, the biggest roller coaster of its kind in Europe . . . the sky riding Pirate Ship . . . the swirling tubes of Snake River Falls . . . the breathtaking Bobsleigh run . . . You might fancy a trip down Nutty Jake's Goldmine to find loads of laughs and nine-carat fun. You can meet furry friends in Playtown's Farm, and choose from a wide range of souvenir shops packed with goodies and gifts galore.

Sometimes it seems easier in Welsh tourism to get a job playing the part of a prehistoric Celt than a contemporary modern Celt. 'Recruits wanted, any age, shape or size, male or female, for a living history reenactment society, recreating the life of the Iron Age Celts from 100 BC to 100 AD', a Tourist Board magazine advertised a couple of years ago, with a (motivating?) photograph of five successful job applicants. Dressed in hessian sacks, with bare feet and flowing locks, they were chained neck to neck, trudging through a wilderness landscape of bracken and scrub birch. They were the Llyn Cerrig chain gang of two thousand years ago.

The bouquet for good cultural tourism goes to the new Celtica theme centre in Machynlleth. There you find comfortable welcoming bilingualism and staff at ease with themselves in Welsh and in English. They have opted for convincing audiovisual displays, and the local employees are spared the business of dressing up out of their own time. Instead there is a fine multimedia presentation of the Welsh Celts, which doesn't stop short at medieval myth, but includes presentations of current cultural life in the locality. Now that is a rare model of culture-friendly tourism, which moreover employs local people all the year round.

'Why do people think the country is for dumping rubbish in?'

Michael Evans, an eight year old pupil of St Padarn's school near Aberystwyth, was staying at his grandad's house in the Ceredigion countryside, and was shocked to discover how many people use the country as a convenient rubbish dump. They have lessons on the environment in primary and secondary schools, but the message does not get through to many grown-ups, who persist in seeing the hedgerows and woods not as wildlife habitats but as handy disposal points for old mattresses and fridges. Michael wrote to his MP, Cynog Dafis:

> I am disgusted with all the rubbish dumped in the Aberystwyth area. Whilst I was out with my grandad today we passed many places where we saw cookers, televisions and radios and many other things.

He got a positive reply from green-minded Cynog Dafis, who confirmed that rural rubbish dumping is now a serious problem:

> Not only does it create untidiness in the countryside, but it also means that valuable resources which could be re-used and recycled are wasted. It is important that Ceredigion County Council develops policies for the re-use and recycling of waste and at the same time have the resources to prevent people from dumping articles of all kinds...

Is there life for the young in rural Wales?

The next generation of rural dwellers are more consumerist and more insulated from the world of nature in their own locality than any previous generation. At the same time they are learning more in school about environmental issues than their predecessors, and they are plugged in to the global electronic village. But, as Cynog warned while opening the Denmark Farm Conservation Centre near Lampeter (a study centre for local children as well as visitors):

> They are less likely to know the names of their local birds and trees, whilst tropical rainforests are more familiar to them than oak woods. They know more about endangered species such as the tiger in India or the rhino, than they do about species around them—the lichens, adders,

newts . . . for local children Denmark Farm has been very successful in changing this. Denmark Farm is a living resource in this respect.

The children growing up now in rural Wales have a chance to be better informed about environmental issues than the previous generation. But will they choose to connect what they learn with the place where they live—its people, its work and its natural habitats? If they do succeed then our future countrydwellers have a chance of getting back in touch with the old nourishing taproot of rural living, which Gillian Clarke summarises in these lines about doing up the old house at *Blaen Cwrt*:

> . . . It has all the first
> Necessities for a high standard
> Of civilised living: silence inside
> A circle of sound, water and fire,
> Light on uncountable miles of mountain
> From a big, unpredictable sky,
> Two rooms, waking and sleeping,
> Two languages, two centuries of past
> To ponder on, and the basic need
> To work hard in order to survive.

The bottom line, though, is that young people mostly do not stay on to become anyone's country neighbours. They leave to find jobs, or to find themselves, or just, in their own lingo, 'To get a life'.

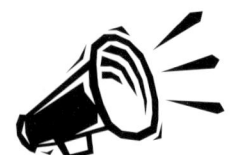

SKIDMORE SOUNDS OFF ABOUT... CITY FOLK AND THEIR COUNTRY WAYS

Nothing would induce me to ring the Mayor of Liverpool and complain that his streets are filthy and probably disease-ridden. The Mayor of Manchester would not thank me for telling him the city reeks of fried onions from the hamburger stalls. And I would expect a dusty reception if I complained to the Lord Mayor of London about the poor devils he allows to sleep in shop doorways. And his tube trains smell like the barrels of badly cleaned sporting guns. So why do city folk feel they have the right to lecture me about the way we live in the country?

When a Manchester private detective bought the Manorial rights of Trefos, my home, he announced he was going to stop shooting, the only growth industry on Anglesey. We have all experienced the city families who come to live in the country and complain about the noise and the smell. The country is a very noisy place. And smelly. Most factories are. If they wanted peace and quiet they should have stayed in their leafy suburbs where the only noise is the crash of a falling lilac leaf or the deafening rattle of milk bottles on a trolley. Hens aren't budgies. You canna throw a blanket over the hencoop and expect them to be quiet. But we always lose. A farmer is forbidden to keep poultry; another can only spread muck four times a year. And the Ministry of Agriculture is funding research in to deodourised manure.

The city folk prancing round in four wheel drives with names like Chieftain and Sabre and Strangler . . . desperately avoiding muddy patches, in immaculate barbour jackets telling us fox-hunting is cruel.

Tell them how a Labour party inquiry found that killing foxes with dogs was the best way of getting rid of them. Explain that gassing is indiscriminate, that shooting wounds more often than it kills. And that means a painful death because unlike a dog there is no antiseptic in fox spittle so gangrene is inevitable. Tell them a vixen has to train her cubs to kill or they will starve. So when they are a month old she moves her earth as near as she can get to a hencoop or a lambing flock. Because they are easy to kill.

But they still say hunting is cruel. Yet they let their own dogs kill our sheep. And fill their luckless pets with so many biscuits the only way to exercise them is to tie the lead to a leg and pull them like balloons.

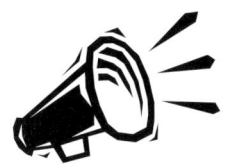

SKIDMORE SOUNDS OFF ABOUT... LOCAL GOVERNMENT, or THE BORDERS OF INSANITY.

Could someone please tell me where I am?

Under the 1974 local government reorganisation Anglesey ceased to exist and Gwynedd took its place. Now Gwynedd has ceased to exist so Anglesey is a county again. Well, that is not quite true. Gwynedd should have become Caernarfonshire and Merioneth but the new Caernarfonshire authority decided Gwynedd, a Welsh name, is more politically correct. So it is going to be called Gwynedd which officially doesn't exist. Then there is Clwyd which used to be Flintshire, though now it is a different and smaller Flintshire than it was. Aberconwy is a county now.

It takes me longer to address a letter than it does to write one. You have to ring the post office in the town to which your letter is going to find out which county it is in. Then you have to find out which post code to use because that can change every few miles. Finally you have to decide which language is appropriate. Do I write Isle of Anglesey or Ynys Môn? And if I write Bangor what then? There are two Bangors in North Wales. In fact there are nineteen round the world and there are plans for representatives of them all to meet in Bangor, Northern Ireland to celebrate the Millenium. My wife says she hopes they have a good map because going to the wrong Bangor would be child's play, especially with all the bilingual road signs.

Maps aren't always a good thing. The new Snowdonia National Park Authority has helpfully put out a map to show us lesser mortals the vast area it rules. Fine except that is has got Pwllheli in the wrong place. According to the map Pwllheli is slap bang in the middle of Llanbedrog.

It's like living in Brigadoon ...

Wales: the People's Landscape

MADELEINE GRAY

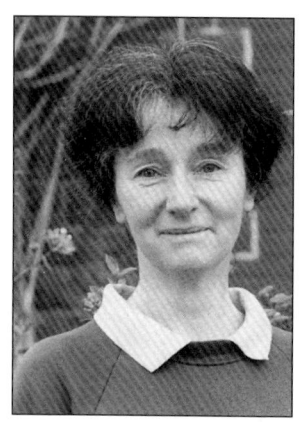

The bones of the Welsh landscape are her mountains, and the valleys which have been carved by her rivers. But the flesh on these bones is the work of the Welsh people —prehistoric farmers, medieval peasants, industrial workers, who have cleared the forests, tilled the land, made roads and villages, dug into the hillsides in search of coal, iron and slate.

The Welsh people have been reshaping the Welsh landscape to suit their needs and priorities ever since the last glaciers retreated. The earliest Stone Age hunter-gatherers reached Wales even before that, in about 225,000 BC. They lived within the landscape rather than trying to change it, though their existence was bound to have some impact. In particular, by travelling with herds of wild animals, they created the first human trackways. They were probably too few to have made much impact on plant life, though recent research suggests that they obtained most of their food by gathering plants rather than hunting.

The landscape was swept away by ice flows during the last Ice Age. As the ice sheet retreated after about 15,000 BC, more groups of hunter-gatherers moved into Wales. They had learned how to build shelters to live in during the harshest weather, and they went on doing this even as the weather improved. These Mesolithic people were still nomadic but seem to have returned to the same settlement sites again and again on a seasonal basis. Many of the known settlement sites are now on or near the coast, like the ones at Trwyn Du near Aberffraw in Anglesey and Nab Head overlooking Marloes Beach in Pembrokeshire. Sea levels have risen since the Stone Age and these sites would then have been slightly inland, but near enough to the sea and coastal marshes for the inhabitants to fish and hunt wildfowl as well as using the resources of the nearby woods. However, there are other settlement sites in the uplands, possibly the bases for summer hunting, like the one at Craig y Llyn overlooking Llyn Fawr in the mountains above the Rhondda.

Pine and birch forests were now spreading across the former tundra. The forest edges attracted wild cattle, deer and wild pig. However, as the pine forests became thicker, finding food became more difficult. The Mesolithic hunter-gatherers had to make clearings in the forests for their settlement sites. It was at about this time that they discovered how to clear larger areas to attract animals to them instead of going out to look for them. These early clearings were partly created by fire, but at least some of the trees had to be felled first with stone axes. The Mesolithic people took forest clearance seriously and were prepared to go some distance for good felling axes. Stone axe heads from Mynydd Rhiw at the tip of the Llyn peninsula in north Wales have been found as far away as Anglesey. Even ordinary axes were surprisingly efficient. Tests have shown that a reasonably fit archaeologist using a typical Mesolithic stone axe can clear an acre of woodland in about two weeks. This compares with a pre-chainsaw clearance rate in modern Brazil of about 2½ acres a month. Limited felling of trees also widened the range of edible plants, since the ecology of the forest edge was far more varied than either heavy woodland or open grassland.

The change from hunting and gathering to farming was a gradual process. From controlling the movements of animals, it was a short step to domesticating them. Similarly, there was a logical development from improving the environment for plants to deliberately cultivating them. There were undeniably outside influences. Farming became more productive and a more attractive way of life when new settlers came to Britain from continental Europe in the 4th millenium BC, bringing with them improved grain crops— emmer and einkorn wheat, domesticated barley—and sheep and goats originally from the eastern Mediterranean. Forest clearance continued, and the cleared land was now made into small arable fields near the settlements and larger enclosures for pasture. It may also have been these settlers who introduced the ard, a simple scratch plough which enabled farmers to cultivate the cleared land more quickly. However, hunting and farming lifestyles probably coexisted for some time longer. It is possible, for example, that hunting groups (the young men of the clan?) used farming settlements as their base, returning with supplies of meat and other animal products. Women were more likely to be restricted in their movements by the rearing of young children. This makes it likely that women were the first farmers: which is why it is so important to talk of a people-made rather than a man-made landscape.

We know little of the houses and settlements of these Neolithic farmers. Those that have been found are on lower ground, near the coast and in the Vale of Glamorgan. They consist of quite large houses, found singly or in small groups, suggesting that agricultural conditions were still far from ideal and that most farming was pastoral. The largest settlement found to date is also on the highest ground, at Rhos y Clegyrn ('the Stone Moor') in Pembrokeshire. Here there were at least seven flimsy stone huts, probably the summer shelters of pastoral farmers based nearer the coast. The most obvious mark which they left on the landscape is their communal burial mounds, which are also found on low ground and were probably near their settlements.

Settled living conditions and better food meant that the population expanded. Fortunately, the climate continued to improve, and it became possible to clear and cultivate higher ground. Burial mounds and other religious sites for this period are found all through the Welsh uplands, on ground which is now far too bleak for cultivation. It is in the uplands, too, that most of the surviving Bronze Age huts and field systems are to be found.

In the hills between Harlech and Trawsfynydd are the remains of a complete Bronze Hill landscape. The route across the hills is marked by standing stones and more complex arrangements of stones and cairns. The ruins of several groups of small huts, all flimsily built, are surrounded by small irregular fields. There are numerous clearance cairns where stones have been hauled laboriously from the cultivated fields and heaped against the walls. On the hill overlooking the settlement is the spectacular burial mound of Bryn Cader Faner.

In south-east Wales no settlements have been identified, but the burial and ritual sites are divided between the coastal plain and the hilltops, suggesting that the steep slopes between had been allowed to remain (or to revert to) forest. Woodland was a valuable economic resource, and recent finds on the Gwent levels suggest that the nearby woods were being carefully managed to produce coppicewood of varying sizes for different purposes. Farming in the hills was probably mainly pastoral and may still have been semi-nomadic, and some at least of the standing stones on natural mountain passes and ridge routes would have guided the seasonal movement of flocks and herds.

Wales in the early Bronze Age seems to have been a prosperous enough place. The climate was benign—rather like Italy today. The land was sufficiently productive to support a growing group of craftspeople. The extensive mine workings on the Great Orme above Llandudno in north Wales produced lead-bronze tools and ornaments of exceptional quality. Trade and communications systems were good: we know of a number of Bronze Age trackways across the mountains, usually marked by lines of burial mounds. There are a number of stone circles and other ritual sites but nothing on the scale of Stonehenge or Avebury, suggesting a largely self-sufficient society of small dispersed groups.

All this, however, was soon to change, as a consequence of the first people-made ecological catastrophe. Tree clearance and overgrazing were beginning to exhaust the thin soils of the uplands. After about 1400 BC the climate became colder and wetter, encouraging the spread of blanket peat and the formation of

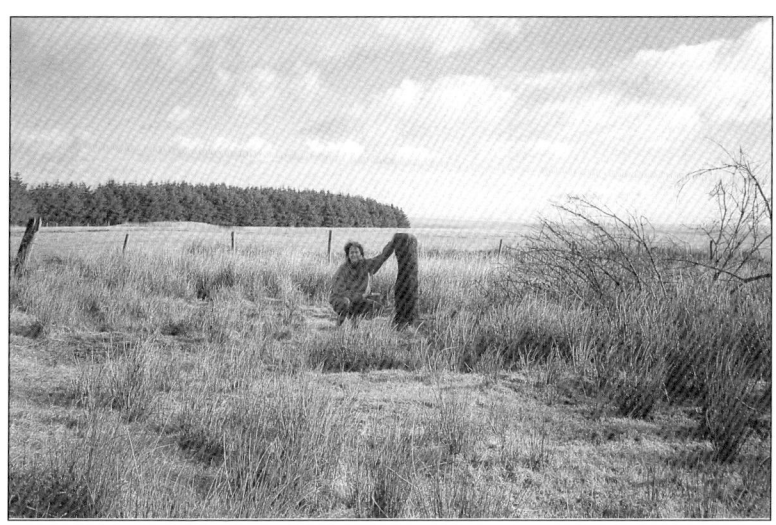

Bodvoc, dark-age memorial stone at Margam

(Photo: S. Gray)

moorland. Meanwhile, the polar ice cap continued to melt and sea level rose, causing floods and the inundation of part of the Gwent levels. Agricultural land was squeezed from both directions. On the better land farmers built fortified farmsteads to defend what they had against refugees from the hills, and organized into larger groups dependent on bigger hill forts. These great hill forts, from Tre'r Ceiri ('the Town of the Giants') in north-west Wales to Lanmelin in the extreme south-east, dominate what remains of the Iron Age landscape. The smaller fortified farms often have widely-spaced banks to shelter a number of animals, suggesting that farming was still largely pastoral, though even the most remote communities would have had to grow enough vegetables for themselves and winter fodder for their animals.

It is more difficult to find the remains of Iron Age fields, but they survive on the slopes around some of the hill forts and farm enclosures. They tend to be rectilinear rather than curved, suggesting organised land division rather than gradual clearance. The field systems on Skomer Island off the Pembrokeshire coast are particularly well preserved. The island had a population of over 100 people in the Iron Age. The foundations of their houses and animal enclosures can still be seen, surrounded by small rectangular fields. The fields on sloping ground are marked by lynchets, the steps formed when soil is loosened by cultivation and slips downhill to pile up against a boundary wall.

This was the landscape the Romans found when they came to Wales in about AD 50, a land of warrior tribes, looking after their flocks and cultivating their small fields from fortified farmsteads. The sheer size of the early Roman fortifications in Wales—temporary camps like the one at Blaen-cwm-bach above Neath, big enough to accommodate three full legions—testifies to the hard fight which these tribes put up. Nevertheless, once defeated, the Welsh rapidly accepted Roman rule, with all its advantages, from improved agricultural techniques to underfloor heating. The more powerful ploughs which the Romans introduced made it possible to farm heavier but more fertile soil. Large villa-style estates of a thousand acres or more spread across the lowlands, and even mountain farms like the ones at Penllwyn near Blackwood and Blaen-y-cwm above Margam show the influence of Roman building design. Arable farming had in any case to expand to pay corn taxes to the army.

Meanwhile, the *pax Romana* meant that fortified settlements like Garn Fadrun in Llŷn could expand beyond their defences, building bigger and more comfortable houses and farming a wider area.

The Welsh also adapted surprisingly well to urban life. The earliest 'towns' were probably little more than native quarters outside the military establishments, with a few squalid alehouses and a couple of young women of negotiable affections. Most towns retained a military element, though on the richer lands of the south there were a few purely civilian towns like Cowbridge and Caerwent. A network of well-constructed Roman roads ran round the coast of Wales, linking the four great forts at Caerleon, Carmarthen, Caernarfon and Chester, with roads like Sarn Helen running inland across the hills, past auxiliary forts and trading centres.

All this came to an end with the collapse of Roman rule at the end of the 4th century AD. The departing legions left a Wales which had been largely Romanized and partly Christianized. The abandonment of Roman towns was in most cases slow and not always complete. The pattern of villa-based estates also survived, for hundreds of years in some areas, though the actual villa buildings probably decayed and were not maintained. What really changed the pattern of settlement was the spread of Christianity. Many of the early churches were monastic and seem to have been founded on land carved out of the estates of the founders' families. This land was inevitably on the edge of the family holdings. As Christianity became more popular and more powerful, further gifts of land to the church eventually broke up the structure of post-Roman estates. Meanwhile, the new churches had attracted settlements around them, settlements which became the new centres of the Dark Age landscape.

The classic example is Llanilltud Fawr, Llantwit Major in south Wales. Here a wealthy Romano-British family had built an extensive villa with fine mosaic floors and an elaborate bath suite. The house remained in occupation for some time but the baths were closed and their furnace converted into an iron foundry. The building then fell into ruins, and the site was used for several formal Christian burials. The local tradition connecting St Illtud with the site is probably inaccurate though impossible to disprove. Nevertheless, St Illtud's great monastery is only a mile away, on what would have been the edge of the villa estate. The monastery became one of the most powerful in the region, and many of the kings of south Wales were buried there. It attracted gifts of land from a number of royal and lesser landowners and replaced the villa as the focus of settlement and land ownership in the area.

Much of what we know about farming and settlement patterns in the Dark Ages comes from evidence about church estates. The traditional picture of free pastoral farmers roaming the hills with their flocks and herds is only one side of the story. On the coastal strip and the richer land of Anglesey and south-east Wales, the Welsh kings and their nobles had land which was farmed by bondsmen, the equivalent of the English villeins, tied to the soil and working the lord's land in return for their own holdings. The village of Llanynys in the Vale of Clwyd still has traces of such a landscape, with a nucleus of well-cultivated land belonging to the lord (in this case the church). Around this are strips of shared land held by free tenants, with pasture in the surrounding moors and the hills to the south-west.

Traditionally, the Normans have been credited with creating the landscape of pre-industrial Wales. Like most traditions, this is something of a simplification. The Normans were great adapters, taking what they found and making it work. The few Welsh entries in Domesday Book suggest that the Normans simply took over the settlement pattern of the lowlands with its bond villages and open fields. It was a landscape which would have been familiar to them from their estates in France. There may have been some forcible re-settlement of English peasants on the Gwent levels as a punitive measure after the Welsh uprisings of the 1090s. The tightly-organised common fields of the levels may date from this re-settlement, or they may be the result of communal effort in the drainage of the fens and the construction of their unique landscape of reens and sea walls. While the Normans took control of the better land along the coast, the uplands remained in Welsh control for several generations longer.

What the Normans did reintroduce to the Welsh landscape were towns. As they fought their way across southern and eastern Wales, they pegged down their conquests with a network of castles. The smallest were little more than earth mounds, but the largest became permanent centres for the government of whole regions. They needed support systems around them—traders to bring in supplies, somewhere for the soldiers to go on a Saturday night. Settlers were attracted to these little towns from England and northern France by offering them extensive trading privileges and virtual self-government, a sort of medieval enterprise zone. Edward I did the same after his conquest of Gwynedd in 1282, founding towns like Caernarfon, Conwy and Beaumaris around his state-of-the-art concentric castles.

Part of the political justification for the Norman conquest had been the reform of the church in England and Wales. The Welsh church in particular was regarded as hopelessly corrupt by continental standards, with a married clergy and monasteries which had become hereditary land-owning corporations. The Normans seized the land of all these institutions and used it to endow reformed monastic houses under their own control. This made little difference to the landscape at first since the new houses they founded were Benedictine, town-based and living off the rents of their estates. However, within fifty years of the conquest, the Norman lords and the Welsh princes were both founding monasteries of a new order. The Cistercians chose deliberately to live in remote areas and preferred uncultivated land which they could bring under the plough by their own efforts. They were responsible for clearing and farming huge tracts of the Welsh uplands. Unfortunately, much of the land they were given was already being used, if only as summer pasture. The Welsh houses seem to have managed to co-exist with the local farmers, but some of the Anglo-Norman houses were not above evicting tenants to create the isolation they desired. Margam in south Wales had a particularly bad reputation in this regard. It is still possible to see the sites of cottages and even of churches which they destroyed at Llanfeuthin near Cowbridge and at Llanegwyd near Bridgend.

It was possible for the Cistercians to cultivate so much new land in the mountains because the climate was improving again. The population grew, and new settlements were established on higher and higher ground. One hamlet on the eastern slope of Cefn Gelligaer north of Caerphilly, on ground which is now rough moorland, had ten houses, including one which was apparently a smithy. The houses, built on small platforms for drainage, were spread out across the slope and were probably surrounded by small enclosures for growing crops, possibly on the infield/outfield system. A plot of land near the steading, the infield, would have been kept under permanent cultivation, well manured and looked after. Other land, the outfield, could be fenced in as needed from the rough pasture and cultivated until exhausted. It was then returned to pasture to recover. Animals could have been pastured on the higher ground. Literally hundreds of such settlements were established all over the Welsh hills by enterprising peasant farmers in the twelfth and thirteenth centuries.

But as in the Bronze Age, disaster was waiting, and the four horsemen of the Apocalypse were ready to ride out. A series of disastrously wet summers in the early 1300s was followed by much colder and wetter weather. Crops could not be ripened, and many of these peasant farmers must have starved. The famine was followed by plague, then by heavy fighting during the Glyndŵr uprising and a savage policy of repression thereafter. The upland hamlets were deserted, and even on the fertile lower land many farmers abandoned their villages for large isolated farms.

Traumatised by over a century of grief, the Welsh people turned to their spiritual life for comfort. The 15th century was a golden age for Welsh religious poetry; it was also the time when many Welsh churches were rebuilt and re-ornamented after the decay of the previous century, and when pilgrimages to local Welsh shrines became increasingly popular. The routes taken by some of these pilgrimages can still be traced, marked by the bases of wayside crosses, by upland chapels and by hollow tracks worn in the ground, over the hills to Penrhys in the Rhondda, along the coast of north Wales to Holywell and eventually to Aberdaron and Bardsey, grave of twenty thousand saints. Above all, they lead to St David's. Twice to St David's equalled once to Rome; thrice to St David's was the equal of the Holy Land itself.

The sixteenth century brought revival and reconstruction. Trade and industry began to flourish again in the wake of the Acts of Union. Seaports like Carmarthen and inland market towns like Welshpool grew and prospered; the population started to rise again and land which had been derelict was reoccupied. There was no improvement in the weather, and the late sixteenth century has been described as a mini Ice Age, when rivers froze over and fairs could be held on the Thames. What made a difference to the farmers was technological change, in particular the liming of acid upland soil to sweeten it. This made it possible once again to grow crops in the mountains.

There were disputes between landlords and tenants as huge tracts of moorland which had been used for rough grazing were fenced and ploughed up. The tenants of Mynyddislwyn, north of Newport, went out with billhooks and staves to break down Thomas Morgan of Rhiwperra's great enclosures on Mynydd y Llan and drove their animals into the wheat he had optimistically planted there. However, the tenants were themselves encroaching on the woods and wastes, taking in a few acres here and there to add to their farms or provide new holdings for younger children. The normal procedure was to take in the land first then reach an agreement with the landlord: and few landlords refused an agreement if it was paid for and a reasonable rent was offered.

Gradually the area under cultivation increased until the maximum was reached in the early nineteenth century. This was the age of Victorian high farming, when huge labour-intensive arable farms covered the lowlands and even rough mountain land was cleared for cultivation again to feed the growing population of the industrial towns. But as the European settlers expanded westward into the American prairie, and as steamships made it cheaper to bring grain across the Atlantic than to grow it here, arable farming suffered another catastrophic slump. Labourers were laid off and left the land to join the industrial population in the towns. It is this which has created the rural landscape we see around us now, a landscape of mainly pastoral farms, growing some crops by highly mechanised processes geared largely to the demands (and rewards) of the Common Agricultural Policy.

In England the eighteenth century was the age of the great house, set in parkland so carefully landscaped that it looked superficially natural. Wales had few of these: our great landowners were most of them absentees, living in England on their Welsh rents. What Wales did have was the kind of spectacular scenery which was becoming increasingly fashionable in the later eighteenth century. Before that time, few had valued or admired wildness and remoteness in landscape, seeing them rather as a threat. But as the landscape became increasingly tamed, people with enough money and leisure to travel began to look for contrasts, for landscape which looked natural but still had a human dimension.

This was the landscape of the picturesque—literally, landscape which made a good picture: forests, towering crags, gothic ruins, but with the smoke from a cottage chimney or a rustic figure in the foreground to give perspective to the whole. Young men on the Grand Tour found such scenes in Italy and the Alps. However, when the French Revolution made foreign travel difficult, they discovered scenery almost as romantic in Wales and the Wye valley. And where the view was not entirely to their taste they remodelled it. Thomas Johnes of Hafod in Cardiganshire bankrupted himself to create an intricately picturesque landscape in the Ystwyth valley. William Gilpin even suggested taking a hammer to the transept gables at Tintern to give them the desirable quality of irregularity. Eventually, though, it was the supremely confident Victorians who remodelled Tintern, evicting tenants from cottages on the site, demolishing part of the precinct wall to improve access, sweeping away the pulpitum screen and the walls between nave and aisles to create the sweeping vista to the great east window.

Meanwhile, another group of outsiders was remodelling the Welsh landscape in a totally different way. Industry had been influencing the Welsh countryside since the first Mesolithic craftsmen found stone for polished axes near Aberdaron in the fifth millenium BC. There were flourishing metal-working communities in the Bronze and Iron Ages, and one of the motives behind the Roman penetration of Wales was to secure control of gold, silver and lead mines. In the sixteenth century the iron masters of the Weald of Kent discovered that south Wales had both ironstone and plenty of wood to make the charcoal they needed to smelt it, not to mention water power to driver hammers and bellows. The arrival of the Mineral and Battery Company to set up a wireworks at Tintern made the Wye Valley a focus for the production of high-quality iron. Workers moved into the area, building cottages on clearings in the forest and creating a classic squatter landscape with smallholdings and little hamlets strung out along a maze of trackways.

We have to remember that it was not the early iron industry with its huge demand for charcoal which destroyed the forests of Wales. If anything, by making woodlands a valuable economic resource, the need for charcoal preserved them for clearance and conversion to farmland. The problem, as always, was a conflict over priorities. If trees were to be coppiced, cut down to stumps and allowed to grow back on a regular cycle to provide cordwood for charcoaling, farmers could no longer be allowed to pasture animals there. There would be no more great oak trees for building, no more fallen wood for fuel, no more taking saplings for fencing and hurdles.

The preservation of woodland thus depended on the determination of the landlord and his willingness to fall out with his tenants if need be. The Earlswood district of Monmouthshire, between Wentwood and Chepstow Park, was solid forest in the early seventeenth century. But the land belonged to the Crown, and the Crown was too busy in the seventeenth century to protect its forests. By the end of the eighteenth century, Earlswood had gone in all but name. Tracks had been made into the woods, small clearings had grown and merged, and the whole area is now another classic squatter landscape. It contrasts with Wentwood and Chepstow Park, both of which belonged to the redoubtable Dukes of Beaufort, and both of which are still woodland.

What really finished the forests, though, was Abraham Darby's discovery in 1709 of a technique for smelting iron with coke. It took half a century for this process to spread to Wales, but it resulted in a shift in the centre of iron production from the Wye valley to the heads of the valleys to the west, where coal and iron seams overlapped. Iron had been produced in these valleys for centuries but the appallingly bad roads meant it could only be brought out by packhorse. Now improved surveying techniques made it possible to build canals from Merthyr and Brecon to the coast. These canals were linked to a network of tramroads running into the hills. The finishing touch came, of course, with the invention of steam trains, the conversion to railways and the construction of huge docks along the south coast.

Sprawling towns sprang up along the heads of the valleys, swallowing up the old villages. Iron production was capital-intensive, and the capital came from outside. There was little concern for the needs of the workforce, or for the impact of industrial development on the landscape. Coal was mined at first to provide coke for iron smelting. The first coal seams to be exploited were on the edge of the coalfield, near the surface and easy to reach with primitive technology. Now at last the thick woods on the valley bottoms were cleared so that pits could be sunk as near to the seams as possible. The mines were small, scattered through the upper valleys, each

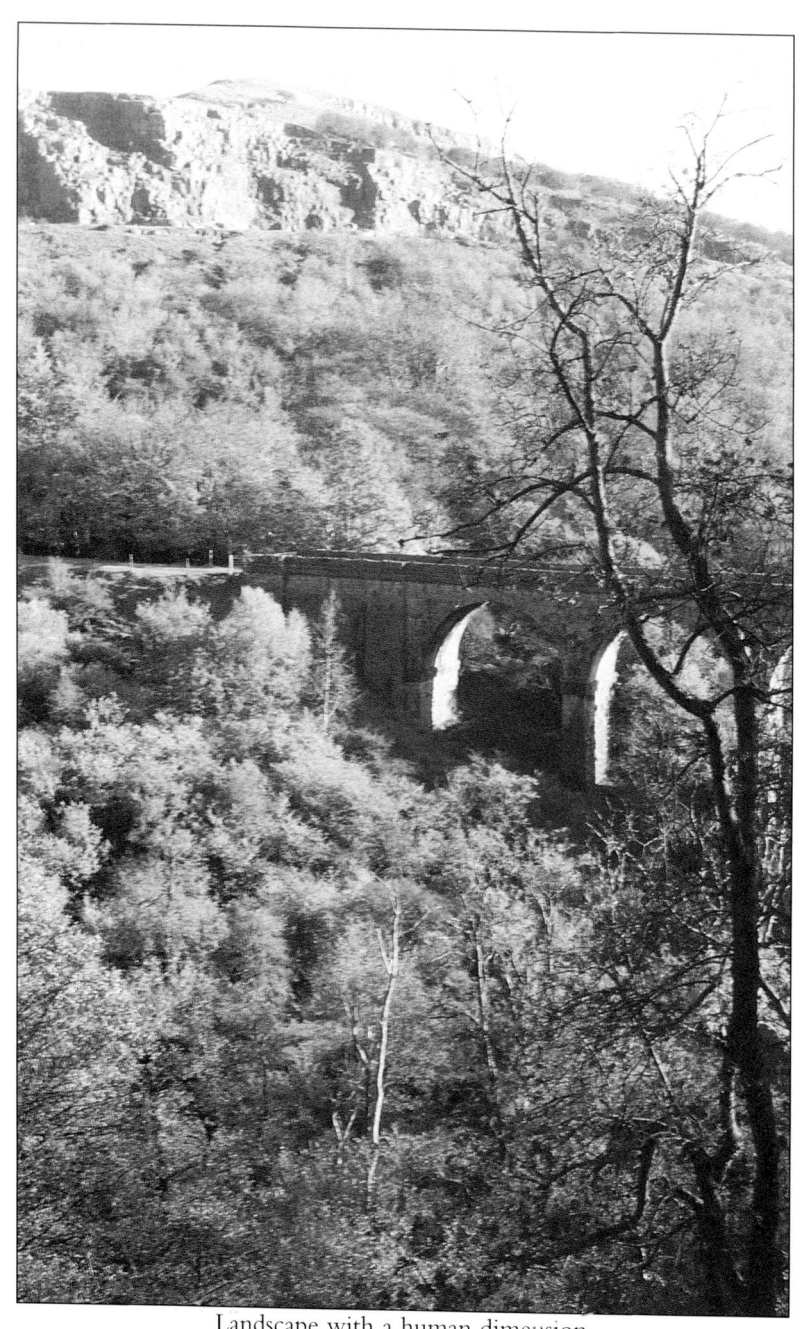

Landscape with a human dimension
(Photo: Erica Williams)

with a huddle of squalid huts for the miners. This was Klondike country: in spite of the efforts of reformers like John Hodder Moggridge, whose model town at Blackwood was based on the ideas of Robert Owen, it took a series of devastating cholera epidemics before the mine-owners and landlords could be persuaded of the need to provide basic sanitation and clean water in industrial housing. The industrial landscape of north Wales is less intense but if anything more awe-inspiring, with huge slate quarries gouged out of the hillsides.

The shaping of the Welsh landscape has always been marked by conflict. Invaders, whether soldiers or industrialists, have imposed their own settlement patterns, their own priorities and preferences. Sometimes the Welsh resisted, with what force we could muster. More frequently we adapted, taking over the new landscape and making it part of our own identity. 'Wales,' said Gwyn Alf Williams, 'exists only because the Welsh invented it.' Now we are taking more explicit control of the making of our landscape, with more clearly articulated ideas as to how we want it to develop. We have new priorities: we value wild and even bleak landscapes, but we get out into the countryside less. While footpaths in the most popular areas are being eroded, others are decaying from lack of use. There is still tremendous potential for conflict. The Welsh Office reserves the power to overrule local planning decisions, imposing opencast mines, out-of-town shopping centres and housing developments on reluctant communities. The old tension between employment and conservation continues: but now there is a new tension between conservation and tourism, between archaeological authenticity and the needs of the heritage industry.

On a more intellectual level, there are splits within the environmentalists' camp. Should we reclaim derelict industrial land, or should we conserve industrial sites as part of our heritage? If we are to reconstruct past landscapes, at which state of the process should we stop—at the heyday of industrialisation, at the carefully-managed arable fields of the eighteenth and nineteenth century, at the scattered pastoral farms of the later middle ages? And how should we people these fields and pastures? Can the recreation of a landscape ever be more than a fantasy, an extended dressing-up game? The heritage industry does not have all the answers. To quote Gwyn Alf Williams again, 'We do not have a heritage. We have a history.'

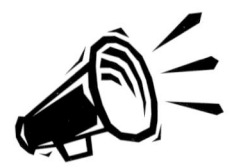

SKIDMORE SOUNDS OFF ABOUT... MUSEUM WALES.

The North Wales Hospital at Denbigh looked after the feeble-minded for over a century. It has closed down now and the patients have been returned to the community. Which sounds a great deal more humane than it is. And the hospital? I read in the *Daily Post* there are plans to turn it into a folk museum.

Everything these days is a bloody museum.

St. David's Hospital in Bangor has closed too. My neighbour who nursed there told me all the nurses think it should be taken over by Marks & Spencer and that is fine by me. But already the lobbyists are saying what a marvellous folk museum it would make.

Glynllifon on the road to Pwllheli is a stately home so grand you could weep for it. Another lobby group is seeking to turn it into yet another museum celebrating Welsh culture. Folk culture, you may be sure.

Some of the glories of this part of the world are the silent ruins of our abbeys. You can walk among the scattered stones of Vale Crucis, stand under the granite skeletons of great windows and wonder what medieval man, so small, with such rudimentary tools could leave such massive memorials to their faith in these silent stone testaments.

Silent? Not anymore. CADW, the Walt Disney of Conservation, is hiring out-of-work actors to dress up as counterfeit Cadfaels and tell rude stories about amorous abbots. Cynan started it. Cynan, the C. B. Cochran of the Eisteddfod and mad Iolo, the drug-crazed stonemason from the Vale of Glamorgan. I may have to leave the country but I have got to say it. Those phoney rituals and absurd bedouin bardic fancy dress have ruined the greatest folk festival on the planet.

But most puzzling of all is this incomprehensible urge to remember our folk history. Why? It was nothing to be proud of. Our folk history is disease and malnutrition. The vicious exploitation of the Snowdon quarries; the ignorance, the pestilence and the wars. We should forget our dreadful history and concentrate on the present. So that our descendants can have what we haven't got. A heritage to be proud of.

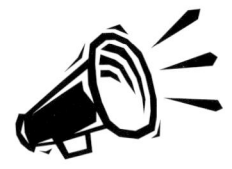

SKIDMORE SOUNDS OFF ABOUT... THE NEW AUTHORITIES

The historian A.J.P. Taylor pointed out that a century ago the only interference the average man endured from the state was prevention of adulteration in beer. Local Government itself only dates from 1880. But my, how it has taken over our lives.

Local government runs theatres at a loss, has departments to advise film makers where to film, factories where to build. It builds its own TV studios, produces its own newspapers. It tells ratepayers not only where to build their houses, but what to build them from. It can even decide the colour paint they must use. And it's getting worse. Even before the new councils came in at the beginning of April 1996 they had spent twenty million pounds in Wales alone building themselves new offices. If paying a wage at all is a betrayal, how much more so are the obscene sums the new councillors have awarded themselves in allowances and expenses. And for what?

Since April 1 the average increase in community tax in Wales is twenty per cent. But not only have the rates gone up . . . the services have been cut. Cuts in schools, fire services, assistance for the poor, the old and the needy. All gone down. Yet Llandudno is to spend eight million on a school for media studies—at a time when there are no media jobs. And Wrexham plans four theatres.

And what do they offer? In Anglesey all taxis have to be white to qualify for a licence. If you think that is silly what about Carmarthenshire? Some councillors want black and yellow taxis; others prefer different colour combinations for each district. In Llanelli white with a red bonnet, the town rugby colours; which means Ammanford having gold for its rugby colours . . . and Carmarthen a rural green . . .

No prizes for guessing who is being taken for a ride.

Incomers

MARIO BASINI

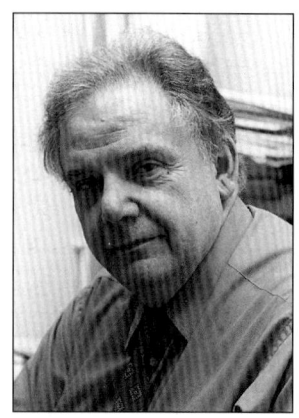

For most of history Wales lay on the remote edge of civilisation, a place as secretive and as forbidding as those vast tracts of unexplored territory over which the ancient cartographers would scribble the fearful message, 'Here Be Dragons'. Much of its territory was hidden behind the tall mountains that walled its interior as securely as the battlements of one of the great castles built by Edward I. Even those visitors undaunted by the terrain have often found themselves discouraged by the cold, wet, wind-swept climate. Yet this small piece of often inhospitable, largely infertile rock has attracted almost as many invaders as the siren call of the sun-kissed Italian landscape. Their arrivals have punctuated the 250,000-year history of Wales like full stops, bringing a halt to one phase of development while heralding the next.

Some have come merely to plunder, others to settle. Many of those who arrived to rob, rape and pillage stayed to create families and settlements and to nurture a future. The influence of most has been benign and creative. Their customs, habits, religions and languages have enriched and expanded Welsh culture, opening up new horizons to those they found here. A few have been powerful enough and hostile enough to threaten the indigenous society with extinction. Usually, their authority has been imposed on the conquered by the force of powerful armies and of potent weapons. But perhaps none has offered a greater threat than the latest breed of incomers, often ageing and physically infirm, armed with nothing more military than money and a few possessions, whose mere presence here could yet engineer the collapse of a culture as old as Europe itself.

The earliest migrations to Wales proved that the influence newcomers exercise over the indigenous population often bears no relation to their numbers. The tall, blond, warrior-like people who settled here around 600 BC came in small clusters. They numbered far fewer than those who took part in later invasions. But such was the superiority of their Celtic culture and social organisation that they quickly stamped their ideas and beliefs on the natives. Their aristocratic system of government, their love of war, their taste for the mystical and the supernatural, their intoxication with words and their love of poetry, even their addiction to drink, played a part in shaping Welsh history 1,000 years later. Their influence remains strong. The offspring of their language still speaks for this corner of the world.

The Celts represented the first great flowering of European civilisation. Their influence spread across the continent from Czechoslovakia and Austria to Turkey in the east, France in the west and as far south as Spain and Northern Italy. Within a few hundred years they were followed into Wales by another great European power which this time managed to hold the known world in its thrall. Like the Celts before them, the Romans imposed a new system of values on those they conquered. Roman law, religion and administration, Roman ethics and military organisation displaced the beliefs of those who had preceded them.

They introduced the British living in Wales to the idea of the town and the city and to the civic duties and responsibilities that went with them. They provided more sophisticated methods of organising agriculture and the economy.

They gave the British a sense of belonging to a sophisticated world state, providing them with chances to prosper by seizing the opportunities for advancement offered by the Empire. Above all, perhaps, they gave them Christianity, the force that played such a vital part in shaping Wales through the centuries down to our own.

But for all their sophistication the Romans never attempted to destroy some of the most important foundations on which the identity of the British in Wales depended. In other parts of the empire—France, Spain, Italy—their Latin tongue quickly displaced the native languages, many of them Celtic. But in Wales, the forerunner of Welsh, Brythonic, was allowed to flourish, its vocabulary enlivened and enriched by generous borrowings from the Latin that are still in everyday use.

It is little wonder that many modern Welsh historians regard the

Roman Occupation as a time when the British culture then prevalent in Wales was enriched and reinforced and the basis for the eventual emergence of a Welsh nation was firmly established. Roman heroes like Magnus Maximus, Macsen Wledig, who led a bid to become Emperor from his base in Wales, played a crucial part in the forging of that national identity. His charismatic figure often appeared in Welsh literature and folklore in the centuries that followed the Roman withdrawal from Wales. He figures prominently in that collection of medieval masterpieces, *The Mabinogion*.

The end of the Roman Occupation in Britain was triggered by the invasion of the Barbarian Angles, Saxons and Jutes who, by the establishment of hostile and powerful English kingdoms, confined the British to Wales and helped to establish a separate Welsh identity. They quickly came to threaten that identity. Not even their eventual subjugation of the proud and independent Welsh could extinguish that nationhood or the survival of a distinctive Welsh language and culture. The heroic opposition of British princes like Arthur helped to establish an uneasy equilibrium between the two peoples. They spasmodically invaded each other's territory. The border between them varied constantly according to which side currently held the upper hand.

That period of precarious coexistence ended with the invasion of the arrogant and imperious Normans who quickly established their dominance over large tracts of Welsh territory. Their huge lordships, sometimes vying with the kingdoms of the native Welsh princes in size, were nominally under the control of the English king. In practice they were independent, with their own laws and customs. Even so, they often served the expansionary ambitions of the English monarchs. It was a 12th century Earl of Pembroke who began the English invasion of Ireland. We are still living with the devastating results of that action.

The Norman territories provided a bridge into the heartland of Wales. An ambitious and unscrupulous English king, Edward I, bent on establishing his hegemony across the whole of Britain, rapidly took advantage of it. The heroic opposition of great Welsh princes like Llywelyn the Great and Llywelyn the Last occasionally succeeded in uniting much of Wales in the attempt to repulse his invasion; they almost succeeded in throwing him and his armies back across the border permanently. But English cunning and military might eventually proved too strong.

With a devastating sense of irony, Edward nominated his own son as the successor to the two Llywelyns as Prince of Wales and built the series of huge castles for which he remains famous. Their impregnable towers and battlements were designed to sit on the Welsh landscape like giant footsteps, crushing resistance underfoot. Wales had become the first English colony.

It was a period when Wales fully experienced the plight of a country at the mercy of hostile invaders powerful enough to impose their will on their victims. It quickly divided into three; the still independent Norman lordships, the domain of the old Welsh princes now under the control of the English king, and the 'Welshry', often the mountainous and unproductive interior, where Welsh laws and customs still dominated daily life. The English established prosperous boroughs, centres of trade and commerce, where swingeing laws aimed at controlling the Welsh often prevented them from living or even trading in the towns. The newcomers took over large tracts of fertile farmland on the plains of the south and the north east.

The divisions were not, of course, rigid. There was a great deal of social interaction and intermarriage between the Welsh and the English. Often, the latter were absorbed into the Welsh way of life. Nor was the Welsh sense of anger and outrage against English domination totally erased. The man who eventually led the Welsh into revolt himself typified the complex relationship between conqueror and conquered that prevailed at the beginning of the 15th century. Owain Glyndŵr was the descendant of one of the most powerful of the Welsh royal families. He was also married to a prominent member of an English family in the border country of Mid Wales where he lived. His English in-laws were among his most loyal supporters when the revolt he led flamed across Wales in the first decade of the 15th century.

The speed with which he rallied most of Wales to his banner indicates the extent of the resentment the Welsh harboured against their English overlords. His revolt devastated massive tracts of Wales. Glyndŵr came close to establishing what Welshmen had dreamed of for centuries: a powerful and independent Welsh state. He held Parliaments, created his own machinery of government, produced far-reaching and imaginative plans for a separate Welsh church and education system. Eventually, perhaps inevitably, the grinding power of the English crown crushed his rebellion and Glyndŵr died in obscurity. The harsh discriminatory laws against the Welsh introduced during the revolt indicated the fear Glyndŵr inspired in the English and the determination of the colonists to keep the Welsh firmly subjugated.

Ironically, it took a Welsh dynasty on the English throne to complete the integration of Wales into the English state. Henry Tudor, born in Pembroke Castle, seized the English crown at Bosworth at the head of his own invading army, many of whom were French. His son, Henry VIII, designed the Act of Union between England and Wales which finally ironed out any differences in law and administration between the two countries.

The influence of the Tudors on their homeland went far beyond the political implications of that Act. Henry VIII's Reformation, for example, and the Dissolution of the Monasteries robbed Wales of some of its finest medieval architecture. The romantic ruins of Tintern Abbey are extensive enough to suggest the majesty of the building as it once stood. But more was lost with the disappearance of the old monastic orders than mere beauty. The Cistercian monks in particular, with their chain of influential abbeys dotted around the mountainous heartland of Wales, had been dedicated supporters of the native Welsh princes and of Welsh-language culture and its achievements in literature and the arts. Their abbeys had become rich repositories of books and knowledge. All was destroyed within a few short years.

The Tudors helped to weaken the traditional supports of Welsh language society and culture in other ways. Their court and capital at London became a magnet for the Welsh gentry eager to seek advancement through the influence of their royal countrymen. They were quick to adopt the mannerisms, the attitudes and the speech of their English counterparts. They frequently neglected their estates at home. When they did return, they often found themselves distanced and alienated from the language and the customs of their people. The strong Welsh ruling class, fiercely proud of its language and traditions, powerful patron of the Bards, the group which had done so much to keep the idea of Wales alive through the darkest periods of English domination, had begun to disappear. This time it was a form of emigration, as opposed to immigration, which had weakened Wales and sapped its resilience.

Not all the invasions Wales suffered were quite so hostile or quite so permanent. The Irish and the Vikings regularly raided Wales in the Dark Ages that followed the Roman Occupation. Occasionally, they left an indelible mark on Welsh history. The names of Swansea and Anglesey derive from Scandinavian words, suggesting Viking settlements there. An Irish invasion in the Fifth century, shortly after the departure of the Romans, helped to establish the ancient West Wales kingdom of Dyfed. The Irish may even have played a part in the establishment of the kingdom of Brycheiniog in south east Wales.

The introduction of Flemish settlers by Henry I into the south of Pembrokeshire to help with the manorial system of agriculture gave the county a distinctive flavour it retains to this day. The Landsker, the ancient dividing line between the Flemish-influenced, English-speaking south and the Welsh-speaking north, remains a feature of the area in the late 20th century.

The most significant period of immigration coincided with the Industrial Revolution and the creation of a prosperous and dynamic new Wales. For a while in the 19th century this small country attracted newcomers at a rate only surpassed by the United States. Migrants poured into its mushrooming towns and cities. Within a few decades Merthyr Tydfil grew from a sleepy rural hamlet with a few hundred people into Wales's biggest town boasting 50,000 inhabitants. Between 1850 and 1914, the population of the twin valleys of the Rhondda, the most famous centre for the production of coal in the world, increased seventy-fold, from 2,000 to 154,000. Even in the north, where the expansion triggered by the Industrial Revolution was on smaller scale than in the south, the number of people living in the slate-quarrying town of Blaenau Ffestiniog doubled between 1851 and 1871.

South Wales in particular became a melting pot into which poured the world's nationalities, out of which was forged a crowded, jostling new society driven by high ideals, riven with low crime, deprivation and squalor. It was a self-confident, high-achieving, outward-looking society, aware of its own ability to climb fresh peaks of industrial achievement and to spearhead the search for social justice and the rights of the working man. It was a time when the sustaining moral values of nonconformism shaped people's lives, helping to boost both the English and Welsh language cultures of Wales. Each made great strides in the south Wales valleys.

It was a time which saw the worst and the best of aspects of environmental change triggered by explosive industrial growth. Huge challenges were successfully met in the effort to house the people who poured into the Valleys even as the steel and coal industries irrevocably changed the landscape by dumping their debris onto it in the form of slag heaps and coal tips. Towns remained sewerless breeding grounds for killer diseases like cholera while great architectural achievements like the ironmasters' folly, Cyfarthfa Castle, classically-designed chapels and the huge, imposing, cathedral-like workingmen's halls rose to dominate the horizon.

From the first the forging of the new and exciting Wales depended to a great extent on the arrival of incomers, attracted here by the prospect of decently-paid work and the opportunities to create a new future for themnselves. Indeed, the Industrial Revolution was largely triggered by a group of vigorous and far-seeing entrepreneurs from England. The Crawshays, the builders of Cyfarthfa Castle, the Guests, the Hills, the Homfrays saw the opportunities presented by the mineral wealth of the South Wales Valleys. They poured their knowledge, their experience and their money into the creation of industries of world importance.

The furnaces they established at Merthyr Tydfil turned the town into the greatest iron-producing centre in the world had yet seen. The Taff Valley became the crucible in which the new society was formed. It quickly spilled over into the rest of South Wales. Many of the newcomers were Welsh, drawn from other parts of the country by better wages and conditions than they could ever expect in the starvation economy of the rural areas. But many were foreigners, attracted like iron filings to a magnet by the dynamism of the Welsh industries. Large numbers came from England, sucked in from rural counties, like Gloucester and Somerset, which bordered Wales. One of the greatest of south Wales miners' leaders, Arthur Cook, was born in Somerset.

Increasingly, the incomers came from overseas. Irish, Spaniards, Germans, Italians, Jewish Russians and Poles, Africans, West Indians, Chinese—all arrived in considerable numbers. The Irish, many of whom were driven here by the horrors of the Potato Famine in the

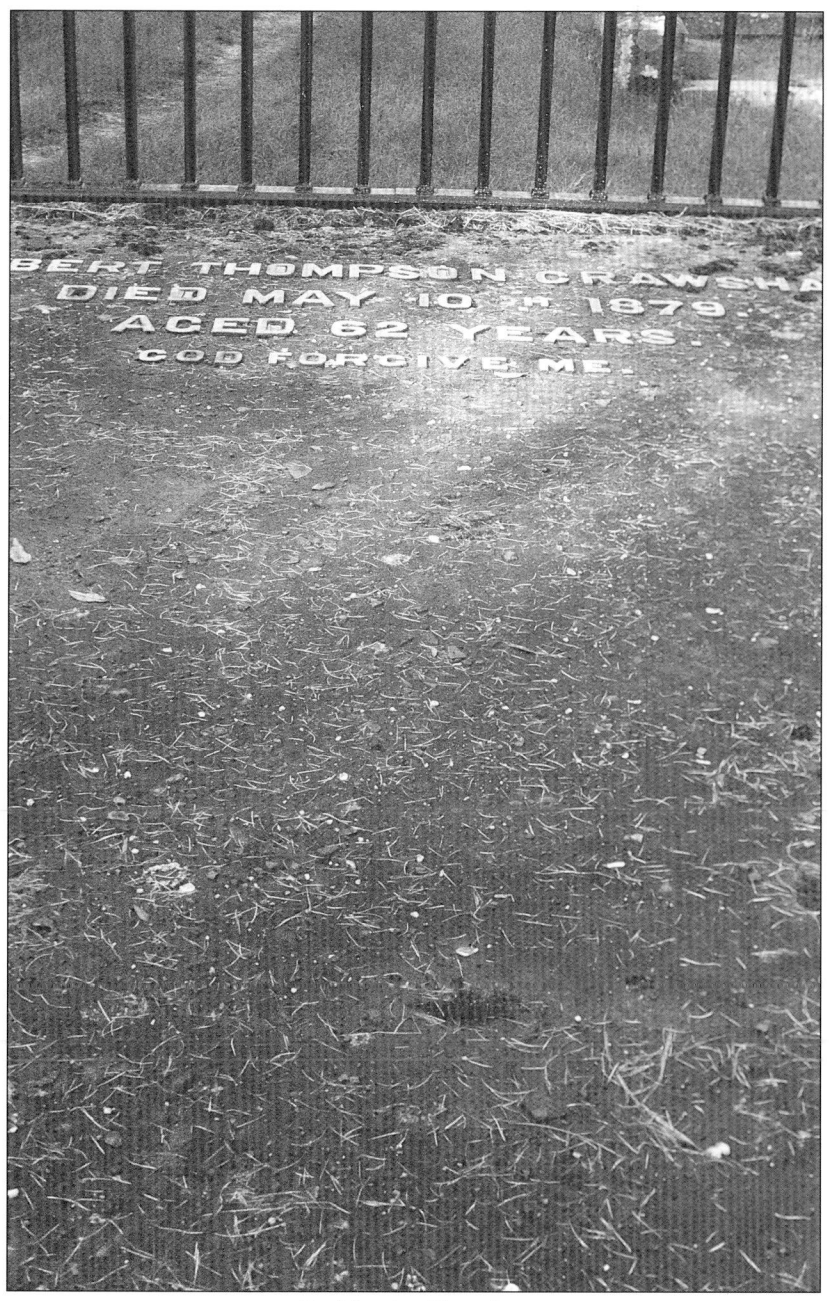

God forgive Crawshay

(Photo: Erica Williams)

mid-1840's, and the Spaniards went to valley centres like Merthyr Tydfil to man the traditional industries of coal and steel. Many were unskilled, carrying out low-paid manual work. But the Spaniards were almost all highly-skilled iron and steel workers from the north of Spain who earned good wages and formed their own distinctive enclave in Dowlais, two miles from the centre of Merthyr Tydfil, which once housed the greatest ironworks in the world. The names of the streets where they lived still bear their signature, like Alfonso Terrace. Many surnames have now been anglicised, but a few like Estabanez and Martinez still bear witness to the distinctive contribution they made to Merthyr's rich racial mix.

Many of the newcomers went to Cardiff which, by the first decades of the 20th century had become one of the world's great ports. Chinese, Africans and West Indians arrived as seamen and stayed to establish their own distinctive presence in the city. They are still largely confined to Butetown, the city's Dockland, locked into what in the view of many commentators has become a ghetto.

My own people, the Italians, provide a colourful illustration of the way in which newcomers were sucked in by the powerful pull of South Wales's prosperity. They arrived here in the late 19th century when the wave of immigration sweeping over South Wales was approaching its peak. They came from the villages surrounding a mountainous small town, Bardi, in the Northern Italian Apennines bordering the province of Parma. For centuries, people from these remote mountain valleys had travelled far and wide seeking work to earn the money needed to supplement the meagre income provided by their small, unproductive, high altitude farms. They went down to the fertile plain of the Po in the summer months to work on the huge farms there. Some took on the back-breaking work of quarrying at Carrara in nearby Tuscany which had once produced the marble for Michelangelo's famous David. Some began travelling throughout Italy selling items like ink or even second-hand books. From the start, their aim was not migration but to earn enough to sustain life at home in the pure air and among the abundant wildlife and beauty of their mountains. The desire to settle abroad only slowly overtook the notion that their forays abroad were temporary affairs. Sooner or later, they would settle back in Italy. Even today, many Italian business people in Wales opt to retire to Italy. And many still spend part of each year back in the Italian mountains. The fact that travel has now become convenient and relatively cheap, the instant communication provided by the telephone and the fact that many have inherited houses back in the mountains only fuel this dual commitment.

When someone at nearby Modena invented the portable barrel organ a new method of earning money opened up to the people of Bardi. They became itinerant street musicians, travelling all over Europe to perform in return for a penny or two from passers-by. Some added performing animals, like dancing dogs or caged mice to their repertoire. Their usual method of transportation was Shank's Pony, but they wandered all over Europe, even reaching Moscow and St. Petersburg. A group of entrepreneurs quickly began to organise the individual enterprise into a methodical business. They employed children, offering their parents legal contracts for two or three years' work. The children were guaranteed lodgings and clothes as well as a percentage of their earnings.

In London the colony of Italians from Bardi and the neighbouring valleys quickly grew. Many saw them as providing a welcome splash of colour to city life. But they also stirred controversy. Critics regarded them as a source of noise pollution. Some, including the great Italian patriot and intellectual, Mazzini, were horrified at what they saw as the organ grinders' exploitation of child labour. When in the late 19th century a new invention, ice-cream, came to the metropolis, they switched en masse from the precarious business of organ-grinding to selling the new confection from handcarts. The streets of London quickly became overcrowded with as many as 900 itinerant ice-cream sellers. The more enterprising among them began to look for new markets. One or two moved to prosperous, bustling South Wales still riding the wave of expansion begun by the Industrial Revolution.

In the South Wales Valleys towns, where often the only forms of recreation were the chapel or the pub, they saw the opportunity for opening small cafes, selling snacks, teas and soft drinks as well as the inevitable ice-cream. The cafes became meeting places, social centres for the surrounding community where revolutions were plotted, love affairs begun, marriages cemented and broken. Each valley town or village soon boasted one. The entrepreneurs, or 'padroni' continued to send home for the children and the relatives they needed to staff their expanding empires. They took their small

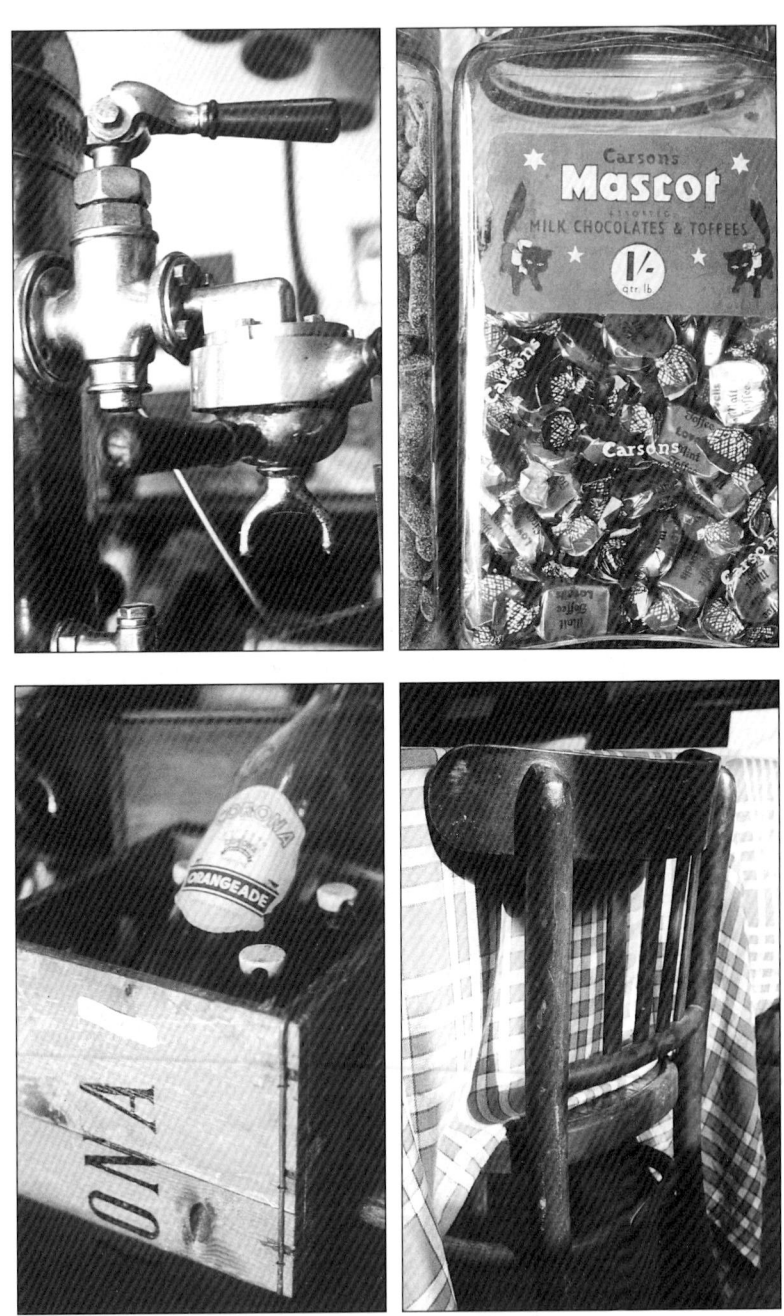

Revolutions plotted, love affairs begun
(Photo: Erica Williams)

businesses throughout Wales. Towns in mid Wales like Aberystwyth, Builth Wells and Lampeter still boast their Italian cafes.

Since each cafe needed its own community of customers to sustain it, the Italians found themselves scattered throughout south Wales. Perhaps because of that and because of their temperamental similarities with the Welsh, the Italians quickly became integrated into local society. These days you will find ice-cream selling families with exotic names who speak far better Welsh than they do Italian. That integration provides support for an idea most of us now accept as fact: that Wales has a remarkable tolerance and lack of racial prejudice.

The record is not as good as many of us would like to believe. Outbursts of anti-immigrant rioting have punctuated the history of the last century. The Italians, so long in Wales that many regarded themselves as more Welsh than Italian, found themselves the victims of violent British xenophobia when Mussolini entered World War II on Hitler's side in 1940. Gangs of rioters took to the streets in several Welsh towns to attack them and their cafes.

Often disturbances, like the anti-Irish riots in Cardiff and parts of the Valleys in the mid 19th century, were sparked by the belief that the newcomers were robbing the Welsh of work and, by accepting lower rates of pay, were undermining the native workers' attempts to improve their lot. Sometimes, as in the anti-Jewish riots in Tredegar in the first years of the 20th century, the disturbances were in part triggered by resentment of the economic power wielded by the incomers. The rioters accused the small Jewish businessmen of being racketeers and of charging extortionate prices in their shops. The major anti-black riots in South Wales in 1919 may have been exacerbated by economic depression and rising levels of unemployment, but they manifested themselves as outbursts of sheer racism and irrational, atavistic fears of black sexuality.

In the view of modern historians, the riots in Cardiff that year, in which three men died and dozens more were injured, led directly to policies which deliberately locked the city's black and coloured communities into their Dockland ghetto. The situation persists today. The community there is plagued by problems of unemployment and crime. Blacks and coloureds are massively underrepresented in the professions and in the media. Serious outbreaks of violence in the Dockland area in 1980's were never reported in the press or on television because of a media blackout imposed by the authorities. Little wonder that those charged with the responsibility of handling the problem are often accused of ignoring it and treating those 1919 riots, like the disturbances of 1980s, as if they never existed.

Even so, Wales can generally be proud of the way it absorbed the incomers who arrived in the wake of the Industrial Revolution and grateful for the contribution they made to its growth. Despite the absolute power they wielded and the huge profits they made from their enterprises, the ironmasters were the architects of the proud and compassionate society that flowered in south Wales in the 19th century. They and their wives were sometimes, as in the case of Lady Charlotte Guest, both cultural innovators and educational benefactors. Lady Charlotte, the translator of that treasure of Welsh literature, *The Mabinogion*, into English was, despite her riches, never too proud to roll up her sleeves to teach the ironworkers and their children who came to the schools and adult classes she established.

Those 19th century immigrants broadened the Welsh outlook and enriched its culture with their different habits, customs, religions and languages They provided a large chunk of the energy that fuelled that period of breathtaking achievement. Would that the commentators in a century's time could say the same thing about the latest wave of immigrants.

In the past 20 years rural Wales has undergone change on a scale reminiscent of the transformation of the Valleys in the last century. Depopulation, the problem that once threatened to turn the heartland of the Welsh language into a green desert, has been halted, even reversed. But the price paid for the victory has been enormous. Far from being based on the growth of indigenous communities, the turnaround has been achieved by population movement on an unprecedented scale. Estimates suggest that as many as half a million people have moved out of rural Wales to be replaced by those of a very different culture, class, and social background. The change has torn huge holes in the vulnerable fabric of the area's social structure.

The young, the talented and the productive have continued to leave their villages and small towns for the opportunities offered by the cities of England or Cardiff and the comparatively affluent south eastern tip of Wales. Their place has often been taken by the retired whose productive lives have ended—no less than twenty per cent of the Welsh population now consists of retired people—or by second home owners who spend just a few days in each week or month in Wales and who remain largely cut off from the indigenous population, cocooned in their bubbles of affluence.

Others have moved into Wales on a mountain of cash generated by the property boom that Lady Thatcher engineered towards the end of her administration. They were able to sell property in England, buy comparable homes in Wales for a fraction of the price and live off the difference. They, too, have often been economically unproductive, contributing nothing to the wealth of the areas they have moved into and little to the culture. They have not been confined to rural Wales. Even Valley villages not renowned for their beauty like Maerdy in the Rhondda have acquired their proportion of such incomers. Often they survive on social security payments once their money has run out.

Some who have arrived in Wales have been idealists drawn here by disillusion with the late 20th century's polluted, overcrowded, distressed urban civilisation. They come in search of a simpler, cleaner, more rewarding way of life. Many of these, too, like the New Age Travellers, have contributed virtually nothing to local economies or cultures. They live in segregated societies, relying on their own systems of self-help and belief in Nature. When they do work, they are often enterprising, building up productive small businesses, for example. But they frequently find themselves out of step with the local society, showing little sympathy for its way of life.

New industries and companies offering services in areas like tourism have moved into rural Wales in the past two decades. But often they are in English-speaking areas, less vulnerable to sweeping change than their Welsh language counterparts. And they frequently bring with them their own workers to fill the key jobs, leaving only menial and poorly paid work for the locals

It is hardly surprising that this massive mobility has led to conflicts between the incomers and local people. One of the most persistent sources of argument has been the vexed question of housing. With prices soaring as a result of outsiders moving in, locals have found themselves unable to afford homes and are forced to emigrate. Critics have seen the Welsh language culture that has developed in rural Wales since soon after the Roman Occupation as the major victim of all this change. What has taken millennia of human endeavour, co-operation, creativity and understanding to develop could be destroyed within decades. The fiasco of the Government's handling of BSE promises to deepen the crisis facing the Welsh language areas by destroying the important beef industry.

The arson campaign against second homes showed how dangerously conflicts between incomers and indigenous populations can develop once left to fester. Yet there is small evidence that even now we are prepared to give the problem the attention needed to produce effective solutions. Academics admit that little detailed research has been done to define the extent of the problem. Even the mildest attempts by planners to tackle some of its adverse effects, like securing affordable houses for locals, are greeted with howls of protest and allegations of racial discrimination against the incomers. Yet to argue that measures against the destruction of the environment are wrong because they contravene the civil liberties of the destroyers would rightly be regarded as absurd in our society. In my view, the cultures and their languages that have been planted and cultivated all over the world—in Scandinavia, Africa, Italy or Wales are at least as valuable as the mountains, lakes, coasts and national parks that surround them. And they are at least as worthy of our protection even if it means—heaven forfend!—placing some restrictions on the working of free market capitalism or on our right to live wherever we please regardless of the consequences.

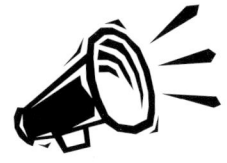

SKIDMORE ON . . . THE POOR TAX

Only a morally bankrupt House of Commons would sanction a State Lottery. It is nothing more than a tax on the poor to provide costly toys for the well-to-do. The Opera House, the super sports stadium, the ambitious horticultural schemes that make the Hanging Gardens of Babylon look like an allotment. And of course museums. And restoration of Houses which have no other virtue than age. All of them toys that much of our society could not afford to play with.

Odd isn't it? We must be the first society outside tribal Africa which won't give medical treatment to the aged, yet lavishes it on bricks and mortar. Only in the rural past of Africa and the American Indian were the old encouraged to go off and die. Here at least we offer them the comfort of a shop doorway or a chilly hovel.

Why not use the money we raise from the pockets of the poor to improve the quality of their lives? A fund for artificial hips for the aged. I know two people who have been turned away from hospitals to die in agony. A fund for that other lottery. The one where you may only get medical treatment over the age of 65 on the whim of a Hospital Trustee. Why not seaside outings for the old? Mass knees-up at Rhyl?

Why not spend some money on the young? In Gwynedd as in other Welsh counties one of our treasures is the youth orchestra. It may not be a treasure we will enjoy much longer. Council cuts you see. Local government is as morally corrupt as the national. So it is impossible to tell whether councils are short of money. Or whether they are cutting where it will hurt the public most in order to bring down the Tories. In Gwynedd the admirable Music Adviser and his staff of peripatetic teachers were all sacked. To be re-employed as freelances at a lower salary. Ordered to fund their orchestras out of fees they get from schools. But schools have no money. Why not poverty tax money to fund that? The gift of music stays with a child forever. Or why not fund school dramas or sports activities? The lottery does not permit that.

Did I miss something? Has someone been shopping for stones on Sinai again? An 11th Commandment; Thou Shalt Not Spend Thy Money on Sensible Things? If the rules say we cannot spend our own money to improve the future of our children or the present of the sick ... Then change the laws. God knows they change every other law they make before the ink on the Act is dry.

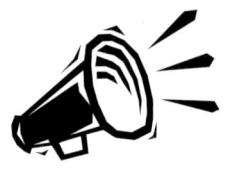

SKIDMORE ON ... THE POOR TAX (AGAIN)

They do say that you can tell what God thinks about money by the sort of people he gives it to.

To see the truth of that you only have to look at some of the winners of the National Lottery. Husbands and wives fall out ... even in one case take each other to court. Friends are betrayed, promises broken. But it's not the effect that sudden riches is having on the poor which bothers me. I worry about the effect it is having on the rich. It is making them greedy.

The lottery reverses the traditional Robin Hood syndrome. These robbing hoods rob the poor to feed the self indulgences of the rich. Botanical Gardens sprouting up all over Wales like traffic cones. Not one opera house but two. Fifty million for a bare face lift at Covent Garden and as much again for the biggest greenhouse in the world on Cardiff dockside. No use asking us here in the North if we approve of the design. A night at the opera in Cardiff for us means a forty quid train fare, meals for the day and an overnight hotel. A hundred quid before we buy the ticket. Why a home for the WNO which can barely afford its present brief visits to Wales? Why not give money to the D'Oyly Carte, perpetually on tour in Wales with not a penny subsidy? Or the Mid Wales Opera?

Why not re-open the country lines that Beeching closed? Stations like that at Glyndyfrdwy, built with voluntary labour.

A million pound Hospice for Gwynedd and Clwyd children has been denied government funding ... Forget Opera Houses ... Mark the Millenium with something really worth having. The Imperial Cancer Fund predicts a golden age of cancer research, saving 75,000 lives a year in 25 years ... if the funds are available. Why not end cancer and the Millenium both in five years?

The money is there. The lottery has brought in two billion with another five million from scratch cards. Three out of four people play, with seventy five per cent it is an addiction. (Up to 200 people in Wales seek psychotherapy). The money comes from villages like Trimsaran in south Wales. It is one of the poorest places in Britain. But its 2,000 villagers are spending an estimated £215,000 a year.

And one final thing. With Government approval Camelot plan to sell scratch cards and lottery tickets in pubs. The law says only games of skill can be played in pubs for money. And writing betting slips is illegal. Alas by making gambling respectable the Government has abandoned the right to control it.

Never mind coffee shops. Wait for the first Casino in a supermarket.

Wales on the Map

JON GOWER

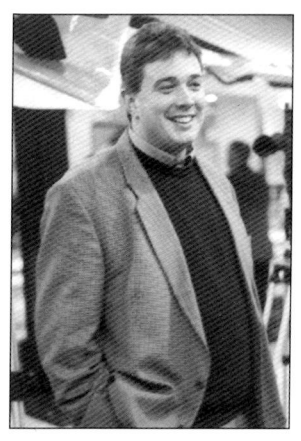

Menna Elfyn's poem, on the facing page, kindled this essay, and is a far more concise 'n' considered version of what will be a more rambling shuffle through a few map rooms, a map-reading exrcise.

The name 'Wales' most often evokes a map in the mind, a geography lesson image of the two peninsular arms of Llŷn and St David's Head reaching out towards Ireland, the uplands shaded in brown, as if the map makers did their work on a brackeny autumn day.

It depends, of course, on which Wales you live in. There are those in the world who live in a different Wales. Like the few hundred who live in Wales, Alaska, only a coracle ride across the Bering Strait from Russia. Or the scattering of towns called Wales that pepper the map of the United States. Or, more improbably, Wales, Guyana, on the northern, jungly rim of South America. It is, presumably, a foetid place, alive with the drone of mosquitoes, where piranha shoal upriver, where one checks behind the shower and inside your shoes in the morning for snakes.

It can also depend on where in Wales you live. In this virtual reality age we increasingly come to lay out our mental maps in filmic images, in three dimensions, or as if we see our world from somewhere on the arc of a satellite.

The very word Wales conjures up a land, a territory, a platectonic eruption, where an 'imagined nation' lives in the shadow of the next millenium. The landscape (and what lies beneath its ridged and pitted surface) has determined the fortunes of the people who live and have lived here. Should some mad scientists hold a phial opening party at the experimental labs at Porton Down, releasing some deadly virus or other and the whole Welsh population was

The Shapes She Makes

I was defining her
on a clean slate,
fleshing out her frontiers,
badgering her to her borders
in red ink;
when a foreign student said,
'It's like a pig running away';
laughing done with,
I believe her;
the northern snout
hoofing it faster
than her southern rump,
fleeing her slaughterers.

She's made of shapes, you know:

the slack old mouth, agape
or the lazy, lolling arm,
resting on its oars;
the jumper, of course,
                half done,
wrapped around a bit of wool and the needles,
or else, she's a pair of scissors
ready to ribbon herself,
an adventurer's double-hafted knife,
or an earthern pitcher,
hollow and cracked.

she's polysyllabled pictures,
this inleted landmass
I swap with acquaintances
and with the foreigner
who sees her for what she is:
comically scattered,
who is,
on my life,
like an unerring boomerang which wills
                      which wills
                its way
            always
        back
     to
  my
feet.   (translated by Elin ap Hywel)

wiped out, the landscape would still be there. There's a saying in Welsh, '*Aros mae'r mynyddoedd mawr,*' which very loosely translates as 'the big mountains remain and will remain . . .' as indeed they will, long after our miserable extinction.

If you live in the lowest corner of south Wales, say on the edge of the Gwent Levels, your map naturally orientates north. From Cemaes, in the shadow of Wylfa's nuclear power station, Cardiff, with its population, its arts, its sense of political epicentre (more if ever we get an Assembly) seems a long way off—five hours at an amphetamine lick by car—or a much longer way in terms of mentality.

Wales was no great shakes on the earliest maps—sometimes just a word, at best the merest hint of a country. On the most famous early map, the Mappa Mundi, safe in its cloistered home in Hereford Cathedral, very little of the country shows up. Medieval cartographers based their maps on hearsay, pilgrims' tales and taller tales. But while you get tall tales in Texas you get small tales in Wales —something to do with our bruised and battered psyche. Maybe it was ever thus.

The very fine Hereford map, compiled towards the end of the fourteenth century or early in the fourteenth by Richard of Haldingham is drawn on vellum and stretched over an oaken frame Two rivers flow across it, the Severn (Sabrina fl.) and (fl. De the Dee). Both seem to rise somewhere in gigantic hills, the present day Clee hills of Shropshire. In north Wales there is mountain mass called Snawedon, which probably refers to the region rather than our highest peak. South Wales is studded with hills but the map reveals itself to be more than a little skewed when one twigs that St.David's is only a few miles—as the raven flies—from Cunwey, or Conway. Maybe ravens flew faster in the age of myth.

By the mid sixteenth century maps begin to show more and truer detail. In the Ezler and Ubelin map, produced in Strasbourg, Wales has graduated to blob-status. Almost as if the map is morphing to coincide with advancing knowledge, the map by Mercator just over fifty years later shows a bud which is Llŷn and the Gower peninsula begins to jut out into the Bristol Channel. By the time one Ortelius of Antwerp offers his version of things in 1595 Anglesey has emerged from the sea and the islands of Bardsey and Skomer are put firmly on the map, or in the sea.

On those early maps there are almost always six rivers. Seteia, the mouth of the Dee (here, nowadays, it is reckoned there is so much heavy metal in the seals that sea-slide around the river mouth that their livers could be processed for mercury on an industrial scale); Tisobis, which is most likely the Conwy, Stuccia being either the Ystwyth, which reaches Cardigan Bay at Aberystwyth, or the Dyfi which snakes past Machynlleth to widen into great bird-haunted marshes north of Ynyslas dunes. The salmon-running Teifi is marked as Tuerobis, the Tywi as Tobius and the tongue-twisting Ratostathybius marks the riverine progress of either the Wye or the Tâf.

Many people are familiar with the 'Cambriae Typus' of Humphrey Llwyd, not least from its reproduction on the cover of John Davies' magisterial *History of Wales*. This sublime engraving is a trilingual map, in Latin, English and Welsh. Present day Newtown's there, as Trenewidd/Newthon, as is Caerdhydh/Cardyff, set in a landscape partitioned into the old kingdoms or '*gwledydd*'—Venoditia (Gwynedd), 'Povisia' (Powys), and Dehenbartia (Deheubarth, a sort of prototype south Wales.) This probably had a bearing on the work of John Speed from Cheshire, whose 'Theatre of the Empire of Great Britain' appeared in 1611. The sixteen town views, mainly of towns with castles, anticipating perhaps the picture postcard

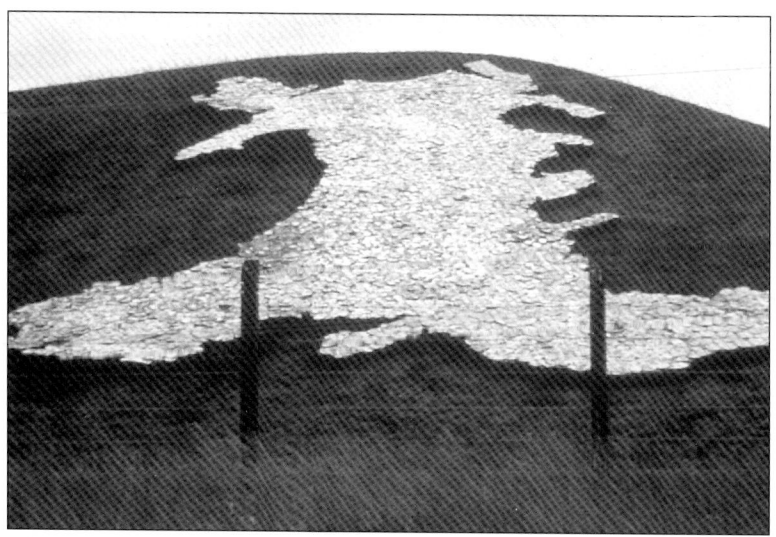

Tin can Wales

(Photo: Arts Council of Wales)

sloganeering of card makers J. Arthur Dixon of Wales as the 'Land of a Thousand Castles'—show four episcopal centres and the main town in each of the shires, not including Monmouthsire, which had been 'pluckt away wholly from Wales, and laid to England, one of whose Counties and Shires, it was from that time forward, and is at this present reckoned.' Here are thirteen counties. Speed surveyed the towns himself but clearly failed to master the art of assessing the height of mountains, with Pumlumon looming much larger and higher than Snowdon.

Another absorbing map is that of Christopher Saxton, the product of his topographical survey of England and Wales in the years between 1573-8. From a distance the parchment face of Wales seems to have a particularly virulent rash, which on closer examination turns out to be a terrain studded with hills, which look as if they have just been pushed up by the velvet snouts of so many moles.

Compare any one the Ordnance Survey's Landranger 160 Maps with these early attempts at Wales-mapping and one gets a sense of how the cartographer's skills have developed, at rapid fire pace. I pick one off my shelf at random. Serendipity—I pause only to remind us that the name derives from the Arab name for Sri Lanka (a place thus giving rise to an abstraction)—takes me to one of the Pembrokeshire maps. It doesn't take long to assemble the very different found-poems of place-names, in English or Welsh, on either side of the Landsker—that invisible line that separates the Welsh speaking half of the county from the southern English-speaking half—a division established over 700 years ago when Anglo-Norman barons and their Flemish mercenaries drove out the Welsh and settled the place with people from Somerset and Devon. South of the line is Studdock, Sheep Island, the Devils' quoit, Rat Island, Sheep island, Rhoscrowther. North of the line—Trwyn Llwynog, Treffynnon, Panteg, Mesur-y-Dorth, Carreg Golchfa and Y Garn. Nowhere is the line more akin to a divide than at Llawhaden and Canaston Bridge, two sides of a linguistic river.

There are other invisible lines in Wales. There is the Mason-Dixon line which defines mid-Wales, which in places can be as thin as a line, separating the industrial south from the mountainous north. According to other maps, say those of the Development Board for Rural Wales, the line is more like a huge swathe of mid Wales, a place of tiny population and many of our eleven million sheep. The tiniest streams define county boundaries, like the trickle of water at Nant-y-Ffin, where Carmarthenshire and Cardiganshire meet at the head of the Tywi valley. There are lay lines and magnetic lines—with maybe a correspondence between the two. I recently spent a delightful day on mynydd Llangyndeyrn, a wild place full of wheatears and bright sulphur-coloured gorse, on the edge of the coalfield and the fertile farming plains of the Tywi valley. Donald Williams, who runs a fire extinguisher business, had pondered many a long moon about the alignment of standing stones on the hill/mountain. One day he realised that the stones ran in a line to a notch in the next ridge of hills, precisely where the sun sets on the 21st December, the shortest day. The calculations were made a long time ago. As if evidence of our forebears' mapping sense and science was needed, a piece of charcoal picked up near one of the '*meini hyrion*' was carbon dated on Donald's behalf by Manchester University, who indicated it to be from 1500 BC, give or take a hundred years.

But there were also mythical maps. Giraldus Cambrensis is reputed to have made 'a map laying down rivers, mountains and sea-coasts, with forty three towns of Wales.' This map is alleged to have accompanied his *Topographia Cambriae* but it's been lost somewhere in the swirling Celtic mists of time. Three hundred years ago that arch Celtic scholar and naturalist Edward Lhuyd tried to track it down but was thwarted. Curiously it was mention of Lhuyd that buried my own optimism about conservation of this wonderful place called Wales.

Guardian columnist William Condry, a wonderful, shy and expert naturalist, told me a tale of how he had been asked by a disabled botanist friend how he might see the Snowdon lily, a near unique and perfect plant of the high Snowdon ledges. Bill took him up on the rack-and-pinion mountain railway which is a hundred years old, stopped the train en route and pushed his wheelchair to the plant. With this single and singular image I realised that there are no real wildernesses left on the map of Wales.

Other maps plotted our myths. My favourite lies between the covers of Eirwen Jones's *Folk Tales of Wales*, part of a feelgood factor series of folk tale collections which appeared just after the Second World War, charged with the same spirit as, say, the Festival of Britain. The map is drawn by Alfred Bestall, the genial creator of

Rupert the Bear, who lived for many years on the north Wales coast. On this line-drawn map Cadair Idris sports its fairy caves and Beddgelert the eponymous, heroic dog who gave up his life to save that of his master, prince Llewelyn's son. Flying fish break surface in the Bristol Channel and on the edge of Cardigan Bay. The longest place name in Wales Llanfairpwllgwyngyllgogerychwyrndrobwyll-llantysiliogogogoch forms a tongue which curls out into Liverpool Bay. There are the dancing and mischievous elves of the Brecon Beacons and the Welsh Atlantis, Cantre'r Gwaelod, a town drowned because of a gatekeeper's negligence. Llyn y Fan marks the remarkable herbalist university of 'The Physicians of Myddfai.' A red hand near the village of Llandybie marks the story of how a drover accidentally beheld a Welsh chieftain, while Merlin's ancient oak in Carmarthen still stands, on this map at least.

A thoroughly gifted successor to Bestall is Margaret D. Jones, of Llanbadarn in Dyfed, whose illustration of the National Museum's 1989 volume *Welsh Folk Tales* is a delight of bright colours; a swirl of red marking the last invasion of Britain at Fishguard when Jemima Nicholas and her friends, dressed in red cloaks and petticoats, confused the French landing force; a grey huddle of cowled figures marking Bardsey island as a place of final rest for 20,000 saints. The frame of the map is alive with rural folk traditions, including the *Mari Lwyd*, love spoons, and harvest plaiting of corn. Some of the tales are bloodily macabre—a skull surrounded by an iron frame denotes the story of Sion y Gof, the blacksmith who killed his wife and two children by throwing them down a lead mine at Dylife, 'because of some other woman and the Devil.' Another motif shows a family walking through a cornfield at Llanllwchhaearn, on the outskirts of Newtown, a beatific crop which magically kept Henry Williams and his Puritan family alive in the face of persecution. Mythical animals abound—the red dragon of Dinas Emrys in Gwynedd, the prophetic eagles which soared over Snowdonia (the Welsh name for this mountain range is Eryri—place of eagles); the Conwy mermaid, the patriotic birds of Llyn Syfaddan—the present day Llangorse Lake—which would only sing at the command of the true Prince of Wales, and the White Stag which was raised at the exact place where Llangar's Church of All Saints now stands.

For a naturalist Wales has generated a fair few maps of real animals which have sadly become the stuff of myth. The felling of the enormous wildwood—a dense forest which covered most of the surface of Wales led to the disappearance of many animals. Once upon a time 90% of the land mass of Wales was covered by trees. By 1980 the Forestry Commission map showed that broad-leaved woodland amounted to little over 3% of the green cover of the land. Conifer plantations cover a further 8% of the terrain. There is some uncertainty whether the brown bear ever padded into post-glacial Wales, although the fact that the name 'Arth' appears in a profusion of place names is suggestive of something pad-footing around. Even as the Normans built their first castles in Wales the wolf roamed and it is more than likely that this slinky creature of the night survived until the sixteenth century. Place names still echo its existence—Wolf's Castle and the Welsh words '*cidwm*,' '*blaidd*,' '*bleiddiast*' and '*bleiddiaid*' are still frequently encountered. Wild boar became extinct sometime round the seventeenth century and by the beginning of the eighteenth century overhunting and overpersecution had pushed the last red deer over the brink. Even by 1188 Gerald of Monmouth avers that the beaver was only to be found in the river Teifi. Nowadays the red squirrel seems most precarious, outposted in a small clutch of forest areas, such as Clocaenog in Clwyd and Newborough on Anglesey.

One of the most complete early exercises in Welsh mapping happened with the Tithe Commutation Act of 1836, when tithes (great tithes payable to the rector and small ones payable to the vicar) were still payable in almost all Welsh parishes. More than two hundred surveyors, on a sliding scale of competence, worked on the maps, followed by a larger army of over three hundred valuers and surveyors.

A look at the old tithe maps of Wales give you some clues about the reason for one bird species' recent extinction. The old system of small fields, cultivated in rotation, is but a folk memory nowadays. Modern agriculture—driven by faceless bureaucrats in Europe seemingly hell bent on building butter mountains higher than the Carneddau and filling wine lakes deeper than Llyn Tegid—led to bigger fields and extended farming into the uplands. Mechanised cutting is one of the key factors in the fate of the corncrake, once described by eighteenth century peregrinator Thomas Pennant as being abundant on Anglesey. Other commentators, such as naturalist

H. E. Forrest, writing as late as 1907, described a similar abundance on the island. Gradually this bird, whose nocturnal call, so much like the sound of two gigantic wooden combs being rasped against each other, used to be such a familiar feature of summer evenings. By 1938 the bird was rare in south Wales, gone entirely from Monmouthshire and very scarce in Breconshire and Radnorshire. Nowadays there are sporadic attempts to nest, sometimes successfully, but the beds of yellow iris which signal perfect corncrake habitat are in retreat. One is reminded that species become extinct not only in the far-flung tropical rain forests but much nearer home.

A sad historical mapping exercise follows the disappearance of the corn bunting, a dowdy bird of farmyards and stubble fields. It went from Glamorgan in 1935, from Carmarthenshire by 1950, and from Cardiganshire in the mid 1930s, when it also disappeared from Merioneth. Nowadays the species clings on precariously in a series of fields on the Cheshire border. The factors are complicated, probably including climatic change. Most recently a Welsh Development Agency plan to create another (as if we need another when so many lie fallow) industrial estate seems set to ensure the bunting's fate in Wales.

Luckily the terrain is still a foil to large scale human development, the scything of roads through the landscape. A plane flight over Wales shows it as pretty much green, a stark comparison with the tarmac swathes that now cover the Midlands, or revealed by a flight into Heathrow, over the concrete expanses of London. This development-hindering landscape partially accounts for the fact that we still have Welsh species, or sub species. The curiously named spatulate fleawort, which blurts its yellow flowers on the headland of South Stack on Anglesey, or the St David's sea-lavender. And unique moth species, like the Welsh clearwing, recently rediscovered.

Some maps were used against us. The National Library at Aberystwyth—run by the extraordinarily helpful Huw Owen and his staff—holds a brightly coloured map of Wales in which the topography of Wales becomes a caricature of Owain Glyndŵr. Gwynedd is his crown, Clwyd his long, moustached face looking out towards England. His cloak, decorated with an unicorn and Aaron's rod, flows down through what used to be Dyfed, that is until another Welsh hero, Sioni Coed Coch, a.k.a. former Welsh Secretary John Redwood recently redrew the map. The caption of this lithograph, called 'Geography bewitched' by Aleph, and produced by Day & Son circa 1869 runs as a rhyme—'Owen Glendower,/In Bardic grandeur, looks from shore to shore/And sings King Arthur's long, long pedigree,/And cheese and leeks, and knights of high degree.'

There was, of course, a long and snide tradition of depicting the Welsh in cartoons riding goats, eating leeks and bearing gifts of rounds of cheese as we went a'courting.

Another lithograph, drawn on stone by the Victorian landscape artist J. J. Dodd, R. A. from a drawing by Hugh Hughes shows north Wales bent scythe-like into the shape of an old woman with a sack on her back. She has an impressive pedigree, being Dame Venedotia alias Modryb Gwen (Aunty Gwen).

The most challenging map maker of recent times was Paul Davies, the Bangor based artist who died on All Hallows' Eve, 1993. One of this selfless artist's most famous works was the mud map of Wales, sculpted by bulldozer in the sodden field of Fishguard's National Eisteddfod in 1986.

Paul Davies' maps were political statements, as politically charged as those maps which show Europe as the centre of the world (these self-same maps are the ones used in African classrooms, leftovers of Empire.) Paul Davies' relief map of Wales, set into the landscape around Anglesey's Llyn Alaw, probably the only genuine piece of 'land art' in Wales, works in four dimensions as time changes this arrangement of rocks and vegetation. It is a big work, some seventy foot by forty five foot in dimension and underlines the scale of Paul's vision.

'Beca', the artist's group he formed with his brother Peter, set out their stall thus, citing the history of 'working the earth, making mounds, raising ramparts, digging out excavations and to extract stone, ore and coal. Some of these interventions by men and women in the environment can be seen as heroic scars.'

Some of Peter's maps are political comments on historical events. The Welsh Not—the heavy wooden token placed around a schoolchild's neck should he or she dare to speak Welsh in school—is rendered as a map of Wales with the words 'welsh not' spelled out in letters cut out from a magazine—stylistically like a terrorist's note or a kidnapper's demand. I always laugh at his 'Scotland, Ireland, Wales without' in which the blue of the sea which surrounds the British

Isles, washes over England completely oblitering it. Paul Davies' 'Slate Map of Wales' shows the great pressures which formed the landscape, the deep fissures, the power of platectonic shift which moved whole continents around and resulted in some of the Welsh mountains being older than the Andes, Alps or Himalayas. Indeed these are rocks which took an unbelievable span of 4,000 million years to form. To some romantics, such as Wynford Vaughan Thomas, the great age of our rocks accounted in no small measure for the feel of this blessed place.

The geological map of Wales, as defined by early pioneers like Murchison and Sidgwick gave the name of ancient tribes to these most ancient rocks. There are the Silurian belts and the Ordovician belts. Most comprehensively, the name they gave to the oldest rocks of all, the Mabria, was the Roman term for Wales itself.

Paul Davies represented a conscious break with the romantic tradition—pushing the idea that the landscape of Wales is not a nostalgic site. Many of his materials were as modern as can be. His sculpture at the Gateshead Garden festival and subsequently recreated at Ebbw Vale was a map of Wales made up of recycled tin cans. His 'Car Crash Wales' was a mangle of metals and there are photographs of this genial and committed artist, oxyacetylene torch in hand and welder's mask in place working on one of his big metal maps of Wales, unwittingly apeing the labours of the men and women who themselves sculpted so much of Wales. His 'Satellite Wales,' clearly inspired by one of the Landsat images of this country from space, is a patchwork quilt of red stripes and yellow swathes. One imagines the 'spy in the sky' satellites orbiting over Wales, feeding the data to those bureaucrats who want to verify the truth of what farmers tell them about the crops they grow and stocking rates. Where the grass grows and whether it is rye grass or marijuana.

Paul never finished his giant Merthyr project—a sculpted earth map of the world with the town at its centre, emphasising Merthyr's historic importance and the industrial exploitation of the earth's resources. This was to be called Mappa Mundi. Full circle.

The poet Tony Conran, a friend of Paul Davies, wrote thus of the 'Heraldic Map of Wales,' which was used to decorate the cover of one of his books:

'I have known some people to be delighted with "Heraldic Wales" as an abstract painting, who then felt disappointed and let down by it when they realised it was a map of Wales. This was to see the picture in isolation, of course. The other maps, if you know them, won't so easily let you forget the mapness of this one. Pop art might have painted a map, as Jasper Johns painted an American flag; but in Paul Davies the image of the map of Wales is often no more than suggested, a sign that he is speaking a particular visual language. Wales is a metaphor as much as a place . . .

'The American flag, or a tin soup can, or even the map of Ireland and the Guinness harp, are pop images in a way that the map of Wales has never been. So Paul Davies is often to be seen as not so much referring to a well-known image as creating it as he goes along. And yet, if that image is primarily a language, a metaphor for how he sees the world, it is also a real place, a human country where real people live and suffer. The human content of his work is irrefrangible because it is tied to what is done and suffered here and now, within the tentative yet complicated border land that we call Wales."

Border land might sound a bit dismissive, but a recent map of the economic regions of Europe underlines how Wales is on the very edge, the periphery of economic activity. Economic success is reflected in the colours ascribed—the Italian powerhouse, Milan and so on, is a furnace red, as are some of the money-generating areas of Germany. Seemingly successful cities like Barcelona are reduced, when they are considered by the full arc lamp of economic scrutiny, to small oranges. Wales is milkily colourless.

Maps are often political acts. Look at a map of Morocco and the disputed areas where the Polisario fight on in the desert heat is often edged in a broken red line. Maps are also unfair. The Phillips projection is just one device for restoring some sense of equity, but the fact remains that most maps in Europe are Eurocentric. American maps likewise reflect the collective egocentricism. Our cartographers tend to set us at the heart of things. One recent set of political acts has been the production of various Welsh maps and atlases—*Y Map Cymraeg o Gymru* (The Welsh Map of Wales) *Atlas Y Cymry* (the Atlas of the Welsh) and *Yr Atlas Gymraeg* (the Welsh Atlas) edited by the indefatigable Dafydd Orwig. But the biggest has to be the National Atlas, masterminded by Harold Carter. Space prevents a full paean of praise. It is one of the most remarkable works of cartographic art and repository of fact in any of our libraries.

Wales has lost its metaphors. A recent report showed that male voice choirs were finding it hard to recruit new voices—the report might be said to have had an urgent tenor! The mines have pretty much gone, with singular exceptions such as the success story of Tower, or the tourist mecca that is Blaenafon's Big Pit. The old energy sources are gone, but the horizon punctuated by oil rigs and the licences for methane exploration where once were coal-pits are the symbols of change. There are now maps which show how we protect our Welsh landcape—in National Parks, Sites of Special Scientific Interest, Environmentally Sensitive Areas, a veritable litany of schemes and reserves. Much as Bell Jar Wales, our careful placing of glass cases around the industry and way of life that once obtained still leaves us looking for what this country's about right now, as we chug towards the cusp of millenia. Paul Davies' maps show one way of marshalling our metaphors. For as Tony Conran says in his poem 'Maps 2' in his symphonic volume *All Hallows* sequence dedicated to the memory of Paul:

> But Wales is like perspective, it describes the space
> imagination is using. As in the inside-out
> perspective of Chinese silks,
> the vanishing point
> is you.
>
> After the twentieth map, you're part of the crowd.
> Daughter of Becca, the gate's waiting.
>
> You're faced with desolation and hope.

NOTES ON CONTRIBUTORS

PATRICK DOBBS. Born and brought up in England. Travelled widely in Ireland, North and South America. Settled in Blaenau Farm, Llanddeusant in 1961 where he farms still. A John Morgan Writing Award took him on cycling tour along the Irish borderlands which resulted in *Here for a Month* (Alun Books). Regular contributor to a variety of magazines, mainly agricultural.

DYLAN IORWERTH. Journalist since 1978, when he worked on a local paper in Wrexham. Political correspondent, BBC, 1983-86. Established the Welsh weekly *Golwg* in 1988 and is now its managing editor. He has edited books such as *Gohebydd Tramor* and the recent *A Week in Europe*. Regular columnist for *Planet* and *Western Mail*.

IAN SKIDMORE. Regular broadcaster on BBC Radio Wales and prolific author. Edited *A Gwynedd Anthology*, wrote a celebrated biography of Owain Glyndŵr, books on maritime history, military histories, comic novels and his autobiography *Forgive Us Our Press Passes*.

ELIN RHYS. Regular presenter of BBC Wales' *Homeland*. Lives in Maesybont near Llanelli with husband Richard and daughter Ffion. One half of singing duo Elin ac Eleri. Director of independent television company *Teledu Telesgop*, based in Llandeilo.

MALCOLM SMITH. Dr Smith is Director of Policy and Science for the Countryside Council of Wales (CCW). He is a regular writer for a range of publications including the *Independent* and *Economist* on subjects ranging from the environment to tourism.

SIMON BARFHAM. Pollution officer, CCW. Grew up and educated in N. Ireland, graduating in Ecology from University of Ulster. In same year awarded Institute of Biology Medal for original research into Atlantic salmon migration. Joined CCW in 1992.

MIKE GASH. Born, brought up and educated in south Wales. Studied natural sciences at Swansea University, transferred to

Bangor University in 1961. Joined former Nature Conservance in 1965 as Warden-Naturalist for Anglesey. Stayed with successor bodies, now heavily involved with CCW's work concerning seas and coastal areas.

JACK DONOVAN. Vice-President of Dyfed Wildlife Trust. Lincolnshire born, spent some time in India. Moved to Pembrokeshire in 1958. Bird recorder for the county since early 1960s. Co-edited *The Birds of Pembrokeshire* with Graham Rees.

MADELEINE GRAY. Dr Gray was born in Blackwood and educated at U.W. Bangor and Cardiff. Co-ordinating tutor for local history in Continuing Education Department, University of Wales, Cardiff. Also lecturer at new University College at Caerleon, specialising in 16th and 17th century religion and politics.

NORAGH JONES. Born and brought up in Belfast. Taught at Leeds Polytechnic. Moved to Cwmrheidol in 1986. Wrote *Living in Rural Wales* (Gomer) and now teaches and writes about women's spirituality. Founder member of PONT which seeks to build bridges between different cultures of Wales.

MARIO BASINI. Born Merthyr, educated at Cyfarthfa Grammar School. Took degree in English at Aberystwyth. Taught for a while before being trained on *Western Mail* in 1967, where he is now a regular feature writer, columnist and literary editor.

JON GOWER. Born in Pwll, Llanelli. Educated Llanelli Boys' Grammar and Girton College, Cambridge. Has worked for BBC, HTV, Apex Trust and RSPB. Former editor *Bulletin of the Welsh Academy*, television reviewer for *New Welsh Review* since 1992.

ACKNOWLEDGEMENTS

The book would not have been possible were it not for the television programme created by Richard Edwards of Element Productions. My thanks go to Richard and his enthusiastic team who work behind the scenes or behind the screens on *Homeland*. Thanks also to Erica Williams, the associate producer, for taking many of the photographs which grace this volume.

Teledwyr Annibynnol Cymru, the Welsh Independent Televsion Producers, kindly agreed to our reproducing Dylan Iorwerth's lecture in essay form.

Menna Elfyn's poem 'The Shapes She Makes' in Elin ap Hywel's translation appeared in *The Bloodstream*, edited by Ceri Meyrick, Seren Books, 1989.

Many bodies have kindly supplied photographs—S4C, BBC Wales, the Royal Society for the Protection of Birds and the Arts Council of Wales.

Our thanks also to the BBC's Keith Jones, Dewi Vaughan Owen and Phil George for advice and suppport along the way.

Mairwen Prys Jones helpfully cast keen editorial eyes over the text as it moved from proof to page on behalf of the publishers at Gomer, and offered useful advice at each and every stage. Diolch yn fawr, Mairwen.